CRAVING HAWK

THE ACES' SONS

BY NICOLE JACQUELYN

Craving Hawk
Copyright © 2016 by Nicole Jacquelyn
Print Edition
All Rights Reserved

No part of this book may be reproduced or transmitted in any form or by any means, electronic or mechanical, including photocopying, recording, or by any information storage and retrieval system without the written permission of the author, except for the use of brief quotations in a book review.

This is a work of fiction. Names, characters, businesses, places, events, and incidents are either the products of the author's imagination or used in a fictitious manner. Any resemblance to actual persons, living or dead, or actual events is purely coincidental. The author acknowledges the trademarked status and trademark owners of various products referenced in this work of fiction, which have been used without permission. The publication/use of these trademarks is not authorized, associated with, or sponsored by the trademark owners.

Dedication

For my family,
who barely saw me while I was writing this book.
I love you.

PROLOGUE

HEATHER

SOME DAYS IT felt like high school was slowly sucking away any individuality I'd managed to hold on to for the past sixteen years.

At least I still looked like me. Half of my head was shaved to the scalp and the other half was lime green. Before that it had been powder blue. Before that—platinum. I could never decide on a color I liked, and why should I have to? There were millions of colors in the beauty supply store just waiting to be opened. I wore what I wanted, applied makeup the way I liked, and generally didn't give a fuck.

But lately… well, I'd begun to think that fitting in would make things easier.

"Hey, Heather?" a voice called from behind me as I stuffed my bag into my locker. "Your name's Heather, right?"

I turned toward the voice and found a kid from my class, who *knew* my name was Heather.

"What's up, Silas?" I asked with a small smile, highlighting that I knew *his* name.

"I was wondering if you want to go out sometime?" He said it so confidently that I had to lock my jaw to keep it from falling open in surprise.

"Go out with you?" I asked suspiciously. "Go where?"

"I don't know. To a movie or something," he replied. His voice had lost the almost cocky tone, changing to nervous.

"You want to take me to a movie?" I replied slowly.

"Yeah, and then maybe..." a sly smile spread across his face just before his tongue pressed hard against the side of his cheek, giving the impression of a blowjob.

"Oh, fuck you, limp dick," I snapped. I jerked my arm back in preparation to hit him in his laughing face, but before I could swing broad shoulders were blocking him completely from my view.

"Get the hell outta here, Sil*ass*," my favorite person in the world ordered, the muscles in his broad back flexing as he pushed Silas down the hallway. "You want a blowjob you're gonna have to find your tiny dick first."

I dropped my arm down to my side and spread my fingers. They'd been clenched so tight they felt almost cramped. I shook my head as Mick turned back toward me, still scowling.

It wasn't the first time a guy had propositioned me in the hallway at school. Shit, it wasn't even the fifth time. I wasn't sure why they'd singled me out, but I knew it was super fucking creepy. I'd turned every single date down. Every single sexual favor they'd wanted. And yet, they still kept coming to ask, like at some point my answer would be different.

"Thanks," I mumbled as Michael Hawthorne threw his arm around my shoulder, pulling me in close to his side as he walked confidently down the middle of the hallway.

Mick and his older brother and cousins were practically untouchable at our school. They weren't super popular or anything like that... but there was just something that set them apart. They were cool. Way cooler than anyone else. And because they were so cool—and in the boys' case a little scary—no one messed with them.

"Did you finish that English homework?" I asked as Mick led me around a group of people clustered on one side of the hall. "You know it's worth like fifteen percent of your grade, right?"

"I got it covered," he answered, squeezing my shoulder. "Why are you always up in my shit about school?"

"Because I'm your tutor."

"Nah, we're friends."

"I'm also your tutor."

"You're a friend that occasionally helps me with my homework."

"See also, *tutor*."

"You wanna hang out after school?" Mick asked, changing the subject as we stopped just outside my next class.

"Oh, not you, too," I joked. I laughed a little until I met Mick's unsmiling eyes.

"Don't lump me in with them," he ordered, his arm dropping away from my shoulders. "That's bullshit."

"Mick," I murmured, embarrassed. "It was a joke."

"No, it wasn't."

I felt my cheeks heat as he stared at me. Mick was two years younger than me, and if that wasn't enough… I knew he wasn't into me. It was clear in every interaction we had. I'd given him every opportunity to make a move, but he hadn't. He'd kept things strictly platonic, never once treating me like more than a buddy.

"I'll see you later," I said quickly, turning on my heel.

"Heather," Mick called in frustration, making me stop just inside the door. "We're cool, right?"

"We're fine," I replied, waving over my shoulder as I moved farther into the room.

He was one of my best friends, and by far the goofiest, kindest, and most protective guy I'd ever met. I wasn't going to ruin our friendship by trying to make it something it wasn't.

After that interaction, I never made another joke about us dating. It wouldn't be until later that year that I'd understand why Mick wasn't into me. I'd find out purely by accident, and I'd never say a word.

Chapter 1

HEATHER

"**T**HE FUCK ARE you doing?"

I opened my eyes and turned my head, looking up at the dark shadow blocking out the night sky. It was big and looming over me threateningly. I closed my eyes again.

"I'm enjoying this little piece of freedom," I murmured, running my arms and legs through the grass like I was making a snow angel. "Grass against my skin, stars above me, I can almost pretend I'm in the field behind my apartment building."

"Christ," the shadow muttered. I heard the flick of a lighter, then got a whiff of the first puff of his cigarette. "You do this shit behind those apartments you live in? Just waitin' around for some junkie to come lookin' for some cash or pussy?"

"That's a poor view of the world around you," I replied, opening my eyes again. "I've never been approached by a junkie, thank you very much."

"Only takes once. What are you gonna do? Fight 'em off with those claws you got?"

"What's wrong with my fingernails?" I snapped, sitting straight up.

"Nothin' if you're plannin' on diggin' up a corpse or some shit. How do you even get yourself off without needin' stitches?"

My jaw dropped open and it took me a minute to even formulate a reply, which then pissed me off more than his question had. "I'm seeing someone," I snapped back. "He gets me off."

"Brave fucker. Wouldn't let those hands anywhere near my dick." His words were so derisive, so disgusted, that I didn't even think before swinging the back of my hand directly at the front of his jeans. Bullseye. For a fraction of a second, my mind registered how big he was even though he wasn't even remotely hard, then I closed down that train of thought.

He dropped to his knees as soon as my hand made contact, and his cigarette got lost in the grass as both hands went down to protect his junk from further attack. I felt triumphant as I waited for him to groan or whine or make some sort of noise, but he didn't. He just sucked in a quick breath, let it out from his nose, and slowly dropped his hands to his sides.

The minute his eyes met mine, I knew I'd fucked up big time.

"I've never hit a woman," he ground out. "But if I was goin' to, that'd be the fuckin' reason."

I scrambled backward across the field until I was sure he couldn't leap out and grab me, then climbed silently to my feet, never taking my eyes off of his face. "That's the only time my hand will be anywhere near your penis." I tried to say it confidently, but the words came out warbly. His dark brown eyes were almost impossible to see in the darkness, but I could *feel* his stare.

"Yeah," he said quietly, climbing gracefully to his feet again as he adjusted the front of his jeans. I forced myself to keep my eyes on his face and not on the motion of his hand. "Didn't want in there when we were in school, didn't plan on getting in there now."

"Like I would have ever let you," I hissed, backing away from him. I wasn't sure how big his balls were, but they must have been massive to say something so ridiculous with absolutely no hesitation.

"Nah, you liked Micky, yeah? Loved that kid." He tilted his head to the side like he was trying to figure me out.

"I don't know what you're talking about," I shot back, fisting my hands.

"I saw all that shit."

"No, you didn't. I never had a thing for Michael. He was too young for me, he—" my eyelid began to twitch. I wanted so badly to punch him in the face. My relationship with Mick was none of his fucking business. It had never been his business. It would never *be* his business. My memories were just that—mine.

"You dug him. Everyone saw it. Everyone said shit," he continued as if I hadn't spoken.

"I-I," the words were caught in my throat as I thought about the boy who'd seen me for who I actually was. He'd seen past the mohawk and the neon blue lipstick. In a school that had a defined set of beauty standards, Mick had been one of the only boys who'd looked at me like I was something special. Not a fetish. Not a chance at freaky sex—because *of course* the girl with the mohawk wanted crazy sex. "We were friends. I tutored him," I said stubbornly, taking another step back.

"You never woulda had him," he murmured back, stepping toward me. "He wasn't into you."

"Fuck you," I whispered, a lump forming in the back of my throat.

"Liked you, sure."

"Shut up," I muttered.

"Thought you were cool, thought you were smart, thought you were funny."

"Shut up."

"Wasn't attracted to ya though."

"Shut the fuck up!" I yelled, my voice cracking.

"You think I didn't know my little brother? You think I didn't *know* him?" he asked quietly, his eyes narrowing into slits.

I froze, my heart thumping so hard I could hear it in my ears. I was so shocked I didn't move as he took a few steps forward and was suddenly just inches from my face. "You get a free pass this time," he said after a moment, like he was doing me some sort of favor.

I swallowed hard as his hands came up, his fingers brushing along the sides of my face until they'd tunneled into the hair by my ears, and he was cupping my head in his long hands. He tilted my head back as the rest of my body stiffened and leaned his face until our noses were almost touching.

"You get one free pass," he whispered again, his breath tickling my face. "You had that one shot and you took it. You don't get another one." His nose slid against mine, and I couldn't help the way my eyes grew heavy. My body was still stiff and unmoving, but every sense was heightened by his presence. I noticed everything—the cologne he was wearing, the gentle way his fingers wrapped around my skull, the way his chest rose and fell with every breath, his wide lips moving so close to mine. He was gorgeous. So fucking gorgeous. And he didn't care. His shirts were always dirty and the mop of hair on the top of his head was always a mess. His clothes usually looked like they'd been slept in and, when he wasn't outside or working, he sometimes wore the ugliest reading glasses I'd ever seen.

It didn't matter. He was still…mesmerizing.

And such an asshole.

And I had a guy waiting for me whenever I escaped from this place.

"Tommy," I warned, pulling a little against his hands. "Let go."

"You know why you get that free pass, don't you?" he whispered against my mouth.

I knew. Of course I knew. But I wouldn't give him the satisfaction of an answer. I didn't keep secrets for *him*.

He tilted my head back even farther, and I automatically grasped his sides to keep my balance. As the fingernails he'd bitched about scratched against the leather cut he was wearing, his jaw tightened and his hands fisted in my hair.

"Thomas, what the fuck?" The loud incredulous voice coming from the back of the clubhouse made me jump almost a foot in the air. "Fire!"

Tommy's hands fell from my head as he spun around, and we both watched in horror as fire spread through the dry grass sickeningly fast.

"Fuck!" Tommy yelled, running back toward the clubhouse as I stood there stupidly. The fire was spreading like crazy in almost every direction, lighting up the grass in small waves.

"I'm gonna beat your ass!" Tommy's older brother Will yelled as they both came running toward me with garden hoses.

"And what the fuck are you doin'?" he asked me as they started spraying water. "Get inside, idiot!"

I stumbled backward as more men came pouring out of the back of the club carrying five gallon buckets full of water like they weighed nothing.

"Girl, you better get outta the way," an older man warned me as he rushed past. "These boys'll run your ass over."

I nodded and shuffled to the side until I was out of the way of their little water brigade. The way they moved, like each one knew what the other was going to do before they did it, was impressive, but it still took them a full twenty minutes to get the fire out. By the time they'd turned off the hoses and were standing around with their hands on their hips, most of the women from inside the club had come out to see what the hell was happening and how they could help.

The crowd went silent as Tommy's dad, Grease, moved toward him, reached him, and lifted him off his feet, hands fisted in the front of his shirt.

"What the fuck were you thinkin'?" he bellowed.

I flinched at the sound, but Tommy didn't move. "Dropped my cigarette," he answered roughly, holding his dad's gaze.

"You dropped your motherfuckin' cigarette?" Grease yelled, shaking Tommy. "We got buckets of water all over the place, and you dropped your cigarette in the dry grass?"

"Yep." Tommy's bored, one word answer seemed to enrage his dad, and Grease dropped him back to his feet, then cuffed Tommy's ear, making him stagger to the side. The sight made everything inside me tighten.

"I hit him in the balls," I yelled absurdly, capturing everyone's attention.

"It's none of your business," my sister hissed, hurrying toward me.

I brushed her off as she reached me and took a step away from the side of the clubhouse where I'd been practically hiding.

"I hit him in the nuts," I said louder, making a couple people laugh. "He accidentally dropped it when he tried to, you know, cover himself."

"Jesus," my sister's boyfriend, Rocky, muttered, shaking his head.

"Why do they always go for the balls?" someone murmured.

"You see that bitch's fingers? Circumcision by fingernail," someone else said.

The crowd snickered and my cheeks burned in mortification.

"What did my son do to make you hit him in the balls?" Tommy's mom, Callie, asked calmly over the laughter. It was the first time she'd spoken to me since I'd arrived at the clubhouse, and my throat got tight as she moved, slowly but confidently, through the crowd toward her son.

"Nothing," I lied, looking over at Tommy. He was watching me with zero expression on his face. I dropped my gaze. "He just—it was nothing."

"It obviously wasn't nothing," she replied, stopping next to her husband.

"He was being an ass."

"Now, that I can believe," Callie muttered, shooting a look at her son. She leaned up and said something quietly to her husband, then kissed him on the cheek. I had no idea what she'd said, but his shoulders relaxed as Callie walked away, not stopping or slowing down until she was back inside the building.

"Fire's out, everyone back inside," the man who'd told me earlier to get out of the way ordered. Without his signature ponytail, I hadn't realized that it was their club's president. Dragon. Stupid name, hot as fuck. Even if he was old enough to be my dad.

"Seriously?" my sister griped as people began to move back inside. She grabbed my arm in a tight hold. "You can't keep yourself out of shit—even here?"

"Oh, fuck off," I retorted, ripping my arm out of her grip. It wasn't like I'd planned it. I'd never be the happy-go-lucky person my sister was. Did trouble seem to follow me? Yes. But I never asked for her fucking help.

"Come on, baby," Rocky muttered, wrapping his dirty arm around Mel's shoulders. He dragged her into the clubhouse along with everyone else and I stumbled back a couple of steps until I was leaning against the wall again. Mel's relationship with Rocky was the perfect example of how differently we were made. He'd been married when they got together. Of course, he hadn't told her that until she was in so deep with him she hadn't wanted to walk away. She let him lead her around, and was perfectly happy with their dynamic. If it had been me? I would have ripped his Adam's apple out with my teeth when I found out he was married. I sure as shit wouldn't have stayed with him, especially considering the life she'd signed up for.

I looked around the almost empty club grounds. All the motorcycles and cars and even a couple RVs were parked out front; beyond some picnic tables, there really wasn't anything indicating we were on the compound of an outlaw motorcycle club. Just grass and trees as far as the eye could see and the lights of a small house twinkling in the distance.

We'd been staying in the Aces and Eights MC's clubhouse for almost two weeks, and I was still trying to navigate my way around. With my sister being a member's "old lady" and our parents out of town on a cruise, I'd been pulled into their lockdown with her. I wasn't stupid, so it wasn't like I was mad about it. If they thought they were keeping me safe, who was I to argue?

But it was hard to understand the dynamics when you were an outsider—and I was definitely an outsider. Mel and her best friend Molly were my only connections to the club, I'd made sure of that after Mick died. I hadn't had any interest in keeping in touch with his family after he was gone. Well, until in an odd twist of fate Molly hooked up with Mick's older brother Will. I'd almost choked on my own tongue when I'd received that little nugget of information. Molly was a nurse, a mom, and completely… normal.

I could totally understand Mel hitching her star to a criminal. She wore rose-colored glasses like a prescription she couldn't see without. Molly, though, she was pragmatic. She knew and understood the score, yet still chose to get back with Will. At least, I was pretty sure they were back together. It's not like they'd made an announcement, though sharing a bed and being connected at the hip were pretty clear indications.

For so many people living in such a little space, the club members and their wives got along surprisingly well. The women bickered and snapped at each other after the first couple of days, but they usually got over things pretty quickly. There was no other way to survive if you were going to be in close quarters for such a long period of time.

The men though… they were harder to figure out. There was clearly a hierarchy. Dragon was the President and Grease was the Vice President, but after that things got kind of hazy. Half of the guys were part of the same family, all married into it in some way or another, and most of them were related to Tommy and Mick in some way. It was confusing as hell, and I couldn't tell who was in charge after Dragon and Grease. Sometimes it seemed like this guy named Casper, other times it was a guy named Hulk that was married to Dragon's daughter. It gave me a headache trying to figure it out.

I'd done my best to stay out of their way for the most part. Their shit didn't have a damn thing to do with me. But as the crowd dispersed and the only people left were Tommy, his dad, the president, and the guy they called Casper, I stepped away from the building again, clenching my fists as I made my way to where Tommy was standing.

"Not your business," Dragon told me gruffly, making me jump. "Go on inside."

"It was my fault," I said hurriedly, lifting my hands palm up. "I got pissed and—"

"Enough, Heather," Tommy said quietly, reaching out to wrap his fingers gently around the back of my neck. "Go inside."

"No, this is stupid." I stuttered to a stop as Tommy's dad stiffened. "It-it was an accident, and it was my fault. I'm the one who—"

"Enough," Tommy snapped, his fingers tightening. "I'll take care of it."

"You shouldn't have to!" I didn't know why I was arguing. The men were scary and they were pissed and I wanted to be anywhere but right there, but I couldn't make my feet move.

Tommy shot a glance at his dad, then before I even realized what was happening he was hauling me against his chest and wrapping a long arm around my shoulders, the other hand sliding into the back of my hair to hold my head steady.

"You're makin' shit worse," he whispered into my ear, his lips rubbing against the skin. "Go on inside. It's all good, yeah?"

"No, it's not," I argued, shaking my head a little. "It was my fault."

"And you'll pay for it later," he snapped back, nipping at my ear. "But not right now. Right now you're gonna take that ass inside and go the fuck to bed."

"What are they going to do?" I asked, my hands digging into his waist where I hadn't even realized I was gripping him. I had no idea why I cared so much. Tommy had been a dismissive asshole in high school and was even more of a dick now, but I just couldn't let it go. We had a history. We'd shared a best friend. For some reason, I felt a loyalty to Thomas Hawthorne.

"Don't worry about it. Just wanna yell at me a bit, yeah? Go on inside," Tommy assured me gently. I didn't believe him. My hands tightened on his vest. Maybe if I stayed where I was they'd lose interest. I knew they wouldn't say or do anything while I was standing there. Their little club was exclusive, and I didn't have a membership.

I inhaled deeply and shook my head, making him growl.

His arm dropped from my shoulders, and suddenly his fist in my hair was jerking my face away from where I'd been pressing it against his chest. "Go. Now."

"Fine." If he was going to be a dick again, he could save his own ass. Jesus, my thoughts were all over the place.

His hand slid out of my hair as he lifted his chin toward the building. God, I couldn't count the number of times he'd done that chin lift thing when we were younger. I'd be hanging with Mick, and the minute Tommy walked up he'd jerk his chin at me, telling me to get lost. It still pissed me off as much as it had back then. I rubbed the back of my head and didn't say another word or make eye contact with any of the men as I spun around. Before I could even take a step, a loud smack sounded right as my ass cheek felt the slap.

"What the fuck?" I cried, swinging my head toward Tommy.

"Said you got one free pass, used that up hittin' me in the dick. Didn't say you could light the whole fuckin' yard on fire," he replied simply. "Go inside."

I opened my mouth to argue and then realized I couldn't. I'd already taken the blame for the goddamn fire.

"Such an asshole," I muttered as I stomped toward the open back door.

As soon as I reached the clubhouse, I paused and turned to look at the men in the yard. I could barely make out their shapes in the darkness, but from what I could see, all of them were turned in my direction, waiting for me to go inside.

Chapter 2

THOMAS

"YOU FUCKIN' KIDDIN' me?" my dad said the minute Heather was back inside.

"Grease," Uncle Casper murmured in warning.

"He coulda burned the entire fuckin' place down," Dad shot back. He turned to me and scowled. "The fuck are you doin' out here anyway?"

"Came out to have a smoke," I replied, clenching my jaw.

"You coulda smoked out front," he argued, "you came out here to fuck around with that girl."

"Does it fuckin' matter?" I blurted, throwing my hands up.

"Movin' in on your brother's girl—"

"What?" Dragon asked, his voice a low rumble.

"She wasn't his girl," I snapped. "Doesn't really matter if she was. My brother's been in the ground for almost three goddamn years."

I didn't see the punch coming, but I'd still expected it. I'd known it was coming since the minute my dad had mentioned my baby brother.

"Jesus Christ," Casper muttered, shoving my dad backward.

"You stay away from her," my dad ordered, letting Casper shove him back another step. "She ain't for you."

I stood there silently as my dad spun on his heel and walked away, Casper following behind him. When they made it back inside the clubhouse, I turned to Dragon.

"That an official order?" I asked, digging my cigarettes out of my pocket like I didn't give a fuck.

"No," Dragon spat, shaking his head. "But you're really gonna fuck shit up with your parents over a piece of ass?"

"Never said I was," I mumbled around a cigarette, patting my pockets until I found my lighter. "But usin' Mick as an excuse for shit is gettin' really fuckin' old."

"Your parents are grievin'," Dragon murmured, walking over to a picnic table and sitting down. "Losin' a kid…" He shook his head.

"Know that," I mumbled, exhaling smoke through my nose. "But Heather? That shit's just stupid. Her and Mick were never together."

"Not what your parents think."

"They didn't even say hi to her when she showed up."

"She didn't say shit to them either," Dragon reminded me, leaning back on his elbows. "Pretty sure they were just followin' her lead."

"Her and Mick weren't together," I said again, annoyed that I found myself defending a nonexistent relationship with a chick I barely knew anymore. "Wasn't like that."

"Don't think it matters," Dragon replied, brushing his hands against his dirty jeans as he stood back up. "They see that girl as his, nothin' you do is gonna change that."

"It's bullshit," I muttered.

"It is what it is," he said, slapping me on the shoulder as he moved past me. "Now take that thing out front before you start another goddamn fire."

I let out a rusty laugh as he strode back inside and glanced down at my cigarette. No way in hell was I going out front to get fucked with by everyone who'd just seen me light the stupid yard on fire. I couldn't believe she'd backhanded me. I'd instinctively dropped my hands to make sure she wasn't going to swing again and I'd completely forgotten about the cigarette dangling from my fingertips.

She'd always been the chick that acted before thinking shit through.

I should have seen the hit coming. She'd be the first person to jump off high rocks at the river, the first one to hang on an old, frayed rope swing. She talked smack to people she shouldn't and gave the finger to pretty much everyone. My baby brother had been the only person I'd ever seen rein her in. After he was gone, I probably should have checked in on her, but I'd been dealing with my own shit.

I pinched out my smoke as I dragged my ass around the side of the clubhouse. There was an RV and a trailer parked near the garage bays with long extension cords connecting them to the club's power, and six tents spread out in the grass for those of us who didn't rate a room inside. Like me. As a prospect, I was a peon at the club still, and I had no idea how long I'd be stuck in limbo. I knew a lot more than the other prospects, it came with being the son of the VP, but I still had to pay my dues. That shit sucked. Especially when I knew shit was going down, but I was expected to stay back at the club with the old ladies.

I shucked my boots and crawled inside my tent with a groan. My balls were still sore as hell. After stripping out of everything but my boxer briefs, I searched through my duffle stored in the corner and finally found what I was looking for. It wasn't like I had to hide it, but with all the kids running around I didn't want little hands finding it.

I loaded up my pipe and grabbed my lighter out of my jeans, and after the first inhale I could feel myself starting to mellow. By the time I was cleaning the pipe out, I knew I'd be able to sleep. Sometimes I couldn't. Sometimes I woke up yelling. And sometimes I had nightmares that left me jonesing for an Adderall the next day so I wouldn't have to deal with them again that night.

I laid back down in my sleeping bag and stared up at the little mesh opening at the top of my tent, listening to people walk around outside. There was a baby crying somewhere, and I could hear my Aunt Farrah talking to someone about a vintage clothes shop she'd found when she and Casper were on the road.

The sounds didn't bother me. If anything, they were almost comforting. They were noises I recognized. Home.

I closed my eyes, and like every other night, I saw my little brother's face smirking at me. Like he'd just done something that would piss me off, but he knew I didn't know about it yet. I'd seen that look a million times when he was alive, and almost every night since he'd died.

"You should ask her out."

"The fuck are you talking about?" I asked, rolling a tire toward our Nova. Some asshole had slashed all her tires in the school parking lot, and it had taken three days to find replacement tires. Such bullshit.

"Heather," Mick said, picking up a tire and carrying it over. "The girls you hang out with are nasty as fuck."

I scoffed. "Doesn't mean I want your sloppy seconds, fuckwad."

"It's not like that," he argued, throwing a greasy rag at my head as I bent down to fit the tire on. "We're just friends."

"Stupid," I called back over my shoulder. "That chick would ride ya like she stole ya."

"Not happenin'," he argued, shaking his head.

"Why not?" I asked, not really expecting an answer. "She's hot as hell."

"See? Exactly why you should ask her out."

"I'm not asking her out."

"You should."

"Not gonna happen."

"Why?"

I stood up straight and turned to my little brother who really wasn't all that little. He'd been towering over me for the past two years, and before that we'd been the same size for most of our childhood even though he was almost three years younger than me. "She wants you, man," I said in exasperation. "She digs you. Follows your ass around, always touchin' you and findin' reasons for you guys to hang out."

"How many times do I gotta say that we're friends?"

"You can say it all you want, Micky boy," I muttered, dropping back down to finish the tire. "But that doesn't make it the truth. Least not on her end."

"Tom!" my brother yelled.

Then I was being tackled to the side as the Nova fell off the blocks. My back hit the concrete hard and the added weight of Mick knocked the breath right out of me. I tried to push him off as I struggled for air, but it only took a few moments for me to realize he wasn't moving. Not at all.

I was gasping for air as I woke up, disoriented for a minute until I realized where I was. *Christ.* I ran a hand down my sweaty chest and threw the top of my sleeping bag off me. Everything was soaked. So soaked, I wondered if I'd just pissed myself. Reaching down, I let out a sigh when I encountered damp boxers, not soaking wet ones.

The conversation between Mick and I had happened exactly as I'd dreamed it. It hadn't been the first time he'd brought it up, but it had been the last. The car hadn't fallen, though. We'd put the tires on with no problem and I'd taken the Nova on a date, got my hands down Ashley McDonald's pants and a stellar blowjob that night.

No, the feeling of Mick's limp body pinning me to the ground was a familiar one, but it hadn't happened that way.

I hopped up and shucked off my boxers, tossing them into the corner with the rest of my dirty laundry. Knowing there was no way I'd fall back asleep, I got dressed in some clean clothes and pushed myself out of the tent. The compound was quiet, and I could see the sun just barely rising behind the clubhouse as I stretched. Might as well get up and get some fucking coffee.

I stepped into my boots and grabbed my smokes, lighting one as I walked toward the front door. All the bays were closed up for the night, but I knew the door to the main room would be open. There was always someone awake inside, especially when we were on lockdown.

"Up early," Poet greeted, lifting his mug in my direction as I stepped inside the clubhouse. His hair was all fucking over the place and his beard was massive, like he'd just woken up, but his eyes were clear and sharp.

"Yep," I murmured, stopping next to him at the bar.

I grabbed a mug and poured myself some coffee as he watched me closely.

"Still havin' bad dreams, are ya?" he asked quietly.

I barked out a short laugh at the way he'd phrased it. Bad dreams? More like night terrors.

"Not so bad anymore," I replied, as I sat down on the barstool next to him.

"Amy's got 'em," he said simply, turning his entire body toward me. "Nothin' to be ashamed of."

"Didn't say I was ashamed."

"Actin' like it, are ya not?"

"Go back to bed, old man," I murmured into my cup. "Your Irish is showing."

He jerked in surprise, then laughed, "Maybe so."

"Her dreams get better?" I asked, meeting his eyes.

"Are the dreams better? Can't say they are," he said sympathetically. "Happens less and less though, as time goes on. Used to be, she said she had them every night. Now, well, mostly happens when somethin' triggers a memory."

"So, the rest of my life then," I barked out a humorless laugh. "Fuckin' fantastic."

"Ah, Thomas," Poet sighed. "Won't always be so fresh, yeah? Time'll dull it a bit."

"I'll take your word for it."

"Your dreams have anythin' to do with that girl with all the shit in her pretty face?"

"What?" I chuckled.

"Uh…" he snapped his fingers a couple times. "Hawk. That's her name. The one that hit you in the cock."

I choked on the sip of coffee I'd just put in my mouth and felt it burn the back of my nose. "Heather?"

"Right! Memory's shit anymore."

"Bullshit. You remember what you ate on February 1, 1982. She's nothin'. Dream didn't have anything to do with her," I lied, wiping the coffee that had spilled down my chin. "She knew Micky."

"His girl?" Poet asked, his tone making my head snap up. He knew something. It was in the way he'd said the words, the way his eyes didn't leave mine, the way his fingers tapped idly against the side of his coffee mug.

"Nah," I replied slowly. "They were just friends."

He hummed in reply, nodding his head.

"She is pretty," I said, thoughtlessly. It was true, but I would have never actually said it if I wasn't trying to steer the conversation in a different direction.

"Eh. If she took that metal out of her face."

I smiled. "She used to have a lot more of it," I told him, watching as his lips firmed in disgust. "She's only got the two now, but she used to have snake bites." I pointed to the corners of my bottom lips. "And she had her eyebrow done and her bridge."

"Her bridge?" Poet asked in confusion.

"Yeah." I reached up and pinched the skin on the bridge of my nose right between my eyes and busted out laughing as he shuddered.

"Well, now," he said, shaking his head. "I'm too old for that shit."

"What? Women didn't have piercings when you were a young fella?" I asked jokingly.

"Only the good ones," his wife, Amy, called quietly as she walked toward us. She wiggled her eyebrows up and down.

"Oh, yeah?" I asked, winking at her.

"No," Poet said shaking his head. "She's fuckin' with ya."

I couldn't keep the grin off my face as Amy moved around Poet and smoothed a hand down his beard, trying to tame it, before she reached for the coffee pot.

"It was all I could do not to pull out every one of the rings your Aunt Farrah put in her face when I saw her. That girl just kept addin' and addin' 'em."

"I don't remember her having that many," I said in surprise.

"Before you were born, son." Poet shook his head and then made a shooing motion so I'd scoot to the next barstool, giving Amy a place to sit down. "She'd mellowed quite a bit before you younger kids came around."

"Having a family will do that to a person," Amy said thoughtfully, lifting her coffee mug to her lips. "Well, most people anyhow. What are you doing up so early?"

"Couldn't sleep."

"I'm sorry, Tommy," she said softly.

"It is what it is. What are you two doin' up?" I glanced at Poet who was grinning from ear to ear. "Don't answer that," I muttered.

He started chuckling just as Heather came out of the back hallway carrying Molly's daughter Rebel. I wasn't sure how my big brother had landed the sweet Molly, but I was a little impressed by it. She was a nurse up at the hospital, and I remembered when she'd come up to me in the waiting room, the night our family barbecue had been attacked, and brought me down to my brother's room. She'd seemed like an angel then, with her smooth blonde hair and soft voice.

I turned on my stool as Heather moved toward us, her eyes bleary.

"I need coffee," she mumbled, rubbing Rebel's back. "Stat."

Amy laughed softly as she reached for another mug.

"What are you doin' with this one?" I asked, reaching out to tickle the bottom of Rebel's foot.

"She slept with me last night," Heather huffed, planting her ass on a barstool with the little girl on her lap. "I didn't realize she'd be up at five in the morning."

"Shit. It's already five?" I said in surprise, pulling my phone out of my pocket to verify. I'd slept almost an entire night.

"*Already* five? Jesus." Heather shook her head. "It's the middle of the damn night."

"Not a morning person?" Amy asked as she handed Heather her coffee.

"Understatement," she mumbled back, smiling. "I need my beauty sleep."

"You look fine to me," I said, making Heather glance at me in surprise.

"Well, I don't feel fine," she replied after a moment, rolling her eyes. "I feel like I got run over by a truck. Did you know that every fucking man in this clubhouse snores? It's like a symphony of snorting and phlegmy breathing all night long."

I laughed hard. I knew what she meant. My dad was the worst, but uncle Casper and Poet played their part, too. I didn't know what it was with old men, but I'd never met one that didn't snore like a bear.

"Sleep in my tent tonight," I said, lifting my coffee to hide my smile when she began to scowl. "Nothin' but quiet out there."

Poet chuckled and Amy scoffed.

"Get the fuck outta here," Heather said dismissively, making Poet laugh even harder. Then she looked down at Rebel. "You hungry, Sparrow? Tommy's going to make us something to eat."

Her eyes met mine, and for a second I was completely frozen. She was giving me shit. Challenging me. But at that moment I couldn't think of a single reason to fight it.

It looked like I was going to be making breakfast.

Chapter 3

Heather

"Seriously?" I whispered to myself as I stared at my phone. I'd been texting with the guy I was seeing, flirting as best I could while I was stuck on the Aces' compound. Life was moving around us like everything was just fine, but tension was building behind the gates. I didn't have any idea what was happening with the boogiemen that were out to get us... okay, that wasn't fair.

I knew the people the Aces were fighting with were bad. They'd killed Molly's dad and beaten the hell out of her. I knew there was something big going on. So maybe they weren't *fictional* boogiemen. But even knowing that the Aces were facing a real threat didn't make the threat seem any more real to *me*. I wasn't even a part of the Aces and frankly, I was sick of sleeping on the floor and being stuck behind their stupid fence all day every day.

I stuffed my pillow farther under my neck and gritted my teeth when it still didn't prop my head up far enough to be comfortable. I was so fucking annoyed. The men were snoring like fucking chainsaws again. It was the whole reason I'd even texted my guy, Brian. I'd hoped that a little conversation would make me sleepy enough to fall asleep again. Instead, I was even more keyed up. I'd texted like I always did, trying to be flirty and sexy, but I'd known by his first reply that something was off. I'd carried on like I didn't notice his abrupt responses, but the last one he'd sent left nothing up for interpretation.

Apparently, we'd never been exclusive, so when I'd left suddenly for

Seattle—that was the excuse I'd given him for dropping off the face of the earth—he'd started seeing someone else. And now he *was* exclusive with her.

Dammit. I'd liked him! He was cute. He had a good job. He was a good kisser. We liked the same movies. I mean, sure, it wasn't like I was ever giddy to see him, or anything like that. But I was getting a little older. I was an adult. I had my own life and too many plans to get wrapped up in some guy.

Someone down the hall coughed loud enough to wake the dead, and I almost screamed in frustration. I had to get out of there.

I crawled out of my sleeping bag and tiptoed out the open door. The room I was sleeping in was filled with all the teenage girls at the club. Apparently the teenage sons could pitch a tent outside to sleep in, but the daughters? Well, they needed their own private space. I hadn't really made friends with any of the girls my age, but they seemed friendly enough. Tommy's little sister Rose was a sweetheart, and so was his cousin Lily. They were quite a bit younger than me though, and caught up in their own little world. His cousin Cecilia was nice, but honestly? She seemed really unhappy. Like, a bone deep unhappiness that didn't seem to go away no matter what she was doing or who she was with. She also seemed to have two guys locked in a cold war over her. It was interesting to watch but I didn't want to get in the middle of that.

The club was mostly quiet, but it wasn't dark as I walked through the main room and out the open front door. They never turned all of the lights off, even in the middle of the night. It made sense, considering the amount of people that walked in and out all fucking night.

I sat down at a picnic table out front and rested my head on my arms. Damn, I was tired. It was crazy how tired I'd been for the past few days. Ever since the night I'd invited Reb to sleep with me, I'd barely been sleeping at all. Not only was it nearly impossible to fall asleep on the concrete floor, but I also wasn't actually doing anything all day so when I climbed into my makeshift bed I was never quite ready to sleep yet. By the time I finally felt my eyes growing heavy, one or more of the guys had already gone to bed and their snores echoed through our room.

The one night I'd shut our door and was able to fall asleep, I'd been woken up rudely by Cecilia kicking me in the side and the sound of Lily sobbing. Apparently, they left the door open for a reason. When I'd closed it, poor Lily hadn't been able to hear her dad when she woke up, and when she'd gone to find him, she'd slammed into the door that wasn't supposed to be closed because she couldn't see it. I knew she was blind, but hell, I'd never been around a blind person before. I hadn't known that was why I had to keep my shit out of the way and my bed in the exact same spot every night. I'd just figured Cecilia was a control freak.

Tommy's invitation to sleep in his tent was becoming more and more appealing as the days went on. We'd reached some sort of truce. We hadn't exactly ignored each other before, but since the fire he'd been more likely to find me during the day and say hello. It was something, at least. It wasn't as if I had many friends in this place. The person I hung out with most was Rebel.

I lifted my head and looked around at the various little camping spots set up. There was no way I'd even be able to find him. If I went from tent to tent, there was a good chance I'd open them to the sight of a pistol in my face, and while I didn't think anyone would actually shoot me... I didn't relish the idea.

I laid my head back down and sighed. This spot would work. I could already feel my limbs growing heavy. The cool night air felt good against my skin after being cooped up inside, and the lack of noise was like heaven.

Sometime later, I jerked awake as I felt myself sliding off the bench.

"Shh," Tommy said softly as he lifted me up against his chest. "You're freezing. Why didn't you come into my tent?"

"I didn't know which one was yours," I answered scratchily.

"The blue and gray one," he said as he walked away from the table.

"What are you doing awake?" I asked, pushing my face against his neck. He was so *warm*.

"Had to piss," he mumbled, stopping in front of a small tent. He set me on my feet and unzipped the side. "Climb in."

I practically dove into his tent, then recoiled when I landed on his sleeping bag. The place smelled like feet. Really stinky feet. With a little moldy cheese thrown in.

"This is disgusting," I choked out, trying not to breath through my nose.

"Quit bitching," he snapped, pushing in behind me.

"This is *bad*, Tommy. What the fuck?"

I heard him zipping up the tent behind me before he replied.

"Have you tried to do fuckin' laundry inside? There's a goddamn line. I haven't had the chance to get in there."

"You haven't washed your clothes in almost three weeks?" I asked in horror, turning to look at him.

"Nah, it's only been one," he said dismissively, lying down on his side. "I threw some shit in with my mom's laundry last week."

"I can't sleep in here," I mumbled, shaking my head. "No fucking way."

"Jesus," he groaned, pushing himself back up. "You're such a fuckin' princess."

"No, I'm not," I argued, pulling my shirt up and over my nose. "No one would sleep in here."

I fell back on my ass as he reached toward me, but he didn't notice as he unzipped the tent again. Then, without another word, he was throwing handfuls of clothes out the opening. In less than a minute, the only things left in the tent were his sleeping bags, pillow, and a duffle bag stuffed into the back corner.

"Happy now?" he huffed, jerking the zipper to the tent closed again.

"It still stinks," I said slowly as he turned to glare at me.

"It'll air out. Now get the fuck in," he said, gesturing to the pile of sleeping bags.

"But—"

"Heather," he cut me off warningly.

I glanced at the front of the tent again, wondering if I should just go back inside and try to sleep there... then an arm wrapped around my waist and I was pulled flat on my back.

"Get under the top one," Tommy ordered gruffly, pulling at the sleeping bag under my ass.

He helped me get situated, and by the time I had a thick sleeping bag pulled all the way up to my shoulder, I finally felt like I could breathe again without ingesting toxic fumes.

"What are you doing?" I asked as he started unbuttoning his pants.

"Not sleepin' in my jeans," he muttered as he arched his back until only his shoulders were against the ground. "I got boxers on."

I was mesmerized as he slid the jeans off his hips and then dropped his ass to the ground so he could pull them off his legs. He wasn't wearing a shirt—which hadn't really fazed me because it was summer and he was shirtless all the time—but that was before he'd taken off his pants, too. Now, I couldn't seem to look away from the muscles flexing in his chest and stomach as he scooted into the sleeping bags with me.

"Come 'ere," he ordered gruffly, straightening his arm so I could slide in against him.

I didn't protest as I curled up against his side. He curved his arm down my back until I was wedged beneath his armpit. For how smelly his tent had been, I was surprised that suddenly all I could smell was clean skin and the hint of some sort of manly deodorant.

"I'm not tired now," I whispered, my eyes wide. I couldn't see much in the shadowy tent, but I couldn't miss his white smile in the darkness.

"Want me to wear you out?" he asked teasingly, his fingers sliding a little farther down my back as he pulled me tighter against him.

"Nope," I replied quickly. I was pretty sure he could feel my heart pounding where it was pressed against the side of his chest.

I closed my eyes as he chuckled softly, the sound almost soothing. Within a couple minutes, I was out.

I WOKE UP to people talking right outside the tent, and laid there for a few minutes, smiling at their comments.

"What the hell?"

"Got tired of smellin' his own stink, I'm guessin'."

"Charlie, don't touch those, baby girl. God only knows what's on 'em."

"Jesus Christ. I really hope my nephew didn't buy those boxers himself."

"Get outta here. Boy hasn't slept in this late for years, let the kid get some sleep."

"It's ten in the goddamn mornin'!"

"And he needs to clean this shit up."

"I'm awake," Tommy growled from behind me, his arm tightening around my waist. "Get the fuck away from my tent!"

Someone started laughing, and after a minute we could hear them moving away from us.

"I told you this tent was rank," I said smugly, relaxing back against the arm I was using as a pillow. Sometime in the night, we'd switched positions, and I could feel the front of Tommy pressed tightly against my back. It took everything I had not to roll my hips against his. I probably should have been embarrassed or something, but I wasn't. It was what it was. I slept in his bed, and we'd ended up wrapped around each other.

Even though most of the time he was a complete asshole, I couldn't really complain. I was warm and cozy; I could hear birds chirping and kids playing. A cool breeze was filtering in through the tent's mesh ceiling, and I had a large palm pressed against my ribs right below my breasts. There were worse ways to wake up.

"Wanna make it even dirtier?" he mumbled, biting down on the back of my neck and making me squeak in surprise.

He rolled his hips against mine and I inhaled sharply. Oh, damn. I hadn't been willing to start that particular game, but I sure as hell wasn't going to turn it down.

"This isn't a good idea," I replied, arching my back just a little so my ass pressed against his hips.

"It's a fuckin' great idea," he argued, his hand sliding up to capture a breast as he ground his hips against me. "All I'd have to do…" His words trailed off as his hand left my breast, sliding down my side until he'd reached my shorts.

His fingers trailed along the waistband for only a second before his hand flattened against my hip. Slowly he smoothed it down the side of my shorts until he reached bare skin. When he gripped my thigh, I let out a small groan and let him pull my leg up and over his.

"Shh," he whispered into my ear as his fingers slipped into my shorts. "You want it, you gotta be quiet."

Someone laughed outside the tent and I froze, but Tommy's fingers didn't stop moving. He smoothed them over the crease between my hip and thigh and then pushed beneath my underwear.

We both groaned a little then.

"Quiet," he said again, chuckling softly against the back of my neck.

"You're making more noise than me," I gasped.

"Lie," he argued. The tips of his fingers ghosted over my skin, barely touching my clit before one was gently working it's way inside me. I was wet enough that it moved in easily, but it only took one slide out and then back in before I was soaked.

"Thatta girl," he praised, making me huff in annoyance. Condescension wasn't attractive… but whatever he was doing with his hand more than made up for it.

I reached back and wrapped my arm around his head as he started to suck on my neck, and my hips moved against his hand in a rhythm that had me panting when he added a second finger. We were cocooned inside the sleeping bag, and I almost forgot we were in a somewhat public place until the walls of the tent started shaking like we were in the middle of a hurricane.

"Get your ass up little brother!" Will called, shaking the tent some more. "Stop beatin' off, we got shit to do today!"

"Get the fuck outta here!" Tommy yelled, breathing heavily as his hand stopped moving.

"Nope." More tent shaking. "Up! Up! Up!"

"Douchebag," Tommy grumbled as Will walked away from the tent. Then he let out a loud sound of frustration against my neck.

"You better go," I whispered, suddenly embarrassed as hell that his fingers were still inside me.

"Fuck him," he whispered back, sliding his fingers halfway out then pressing them quickly back in. "At least one of us is gettin' off."

"Not happening—" I started to say, then let out a deep breath as the hand that had been resting near my face twisted and reached down, pinching my nipple through my shirt without fanfare.

"You'll come, but it's gotta be fast," he said so softly that I barely heard him. "Okay?"

I nodded and closed my eyes, biting my lips to keep any noise from escaping. He knew exactly what he was doing. Exactly how much pressure to exert. He pressed his hips against my ass in time with every thrust of his fingers and frantically pulled at my shirt until it was bunched above one breast.

"At some point, this is gonna be in my mouth," he said as he ran his hand over my bare breast. He lifted his fingers toward my mouth. "Get 'em wet."

My heart was beating frantically in my chest as more noise came from outside the tent, but I followed his orders, sucking his fingers into my mouth.

"Ah, shit," he groaned, biting down on my earlobe. He pulled his fingers from my mouth and brought them back to my nipple, and the new sensation made my entire body tighten.

"You gotta come," Tommy whispered, his thumb finding my clit as his fingers continued to thrust. "You gotta come right now, Heather."

His thumb pressed down harder and harder as it shifted from side to side and suddenly I was there, coming all over his hand as every muscle in my body locked up tight.

His hands kept moving gently until I relaxed against him, then he slowly pulled his fingers out of my shorts.

"Oh, hell," I muttered as I slid my hand down the back of his head and then dropped it down in front of me. "What was that?"

"That was one hell of an orgasm," he murmured back, lifting his head away from me. I felt cold air waft over the spot where he'd been and I shivered. "Damn, you taste good."

I whipped my head around to find him pulling his fingers out of his mouth.

"You need to go out there," I hissed. I was still riding the high from my orgasm, but I knew that if he didn't get out of bed someone was going to come looking for him again, and I really didn't want them to open up the tent and find us canoodling.

"Can't," he replied easily. "I'd poke someone's eye out." He shifted his hips and the erection I'd been grinding against slid between my ass cheeks, a few layers of fabric the only thing separating us.

"Fine," I retorted, throwing the sleeping bag off me. "I'll get up."

I automatically regretted the movement when the cool air hit me, but I didn't let it stop me from crawling toward the tent's opening and unzipping it. Tommy laughed lazily as I yelped at the frigid air I'd let into the tent, but he didn't move as I got to my feet outside.

"Ugh," I said in disgust as I looked around at the dirty clothes covering the ground outside the tent. "You're seriously disgusting," I called, making him laugh again.

I picked up the pants and underwear and socks and t-shirts, working my way around the front of the tent with a scowl on my face. All of it needed to be washed. Hell, some of it was almost stiff with grime.

When I'd picked every piece up and finally held it securely in my arms, I looked up and froze.

Callie was standing there with a surprised look on her face, and her husband was glaring at me from right behind her.

Shit.

Chapter 4

THOMAS

I WAS SO hard it was painful. I'd been hoping that once Heather left the tent my dick would start to behave himself, but that wasn't happening. The blankets still smelled like her. I still smelled like her.

I kicked the sleeping bag down to my feet and groaned. If anything, staying in the tent might've been making it worse.

"Hi, Heather," my mom greeted outside the tent.

Well, that deflated things pretty damn quickly.

I sat up and reached for my pants as Heather said an embarrassed hello, but I didn't hurry. It was kind of funny listening to her try to act like she hadn't just climbed out of my bed. She mumbled something about the weather and I had to swallow back a laugh.

I'd always known she was hot. Even when half of her head was shaved and the rest of it was waxed into a blue mohawk, she'd still been shit hot. The way she moved, the way she looked at me, her attitude, her ass, all of it was damn near made to make my dick hard. But I hadn't really realized how cute she was until I heard her stumbling over her words.

"You makin' a comparison?" a low voice asked.

My dad.

That motherfucker.

I didn't bother with a shirt as I stepped quickly through the tent opening.

"What?" Heather asked in confusion. She took a step back, though.

She knew whatever he was saying was fucked.

"First one Hawthorne, then the other," my dad replied. "Will's got an old lady, not gonna get in there."

"Shut your fuckin' mouth," I growled, stepping in front of Heather. "Don't talk to her like that."

"Asa," my mom said in disgust, elbowing him in the stomach. "You're being an asshole."

"Wait," Heather drawled from behind me before taking a step to the side so she could see my dad. "You think I banged Micky?"

I glanced at my mom to find her smiling slightly at Heather's use of my brother's family nickname.

Heather laughed, and my dad stood up straight. *Christ.*

"He was fourteen," she said incredulously. "I was sixteen."

"And?" my dad asked snidely.

"Asa," my mom said again, turning her head to look up at him.

"And?" Heather took a step forward and I moved with her. The girl didn't have a single ounce of self-preservation. "I didn't fuck your son," she said flatly. She glanced at me briefly. "Either of them."

She turned on her heel and tried to storm off, but what looked like a tangled pair of my boxers fell from the pile in her arms and she had to bend over to get it, totally ruining her exit.

"I like her," my mom said, laughing quietly.

"You got no loyalty for your brother?" my dad asked me, completely ignoring my mom.

"The fuck are you even talkin' about?" I snapped back. "Her and Mick were friends."

I wanted to point out that my baby brother was fucking dead. He didn't care about any of it anymore, but out of respect for my mom I slammed my mouth shut. That would just hurt her. It would hurt her even more if my dad took a swing at me, and I knew he would.

"Your brother spent every fuckin' minute that he wasn't with you with her," he growled back. "Don't try and bullshit me."

"I'm not doin' shit," I said, running my hand over the back of my head, where Heather had dug her nails into my scalp.

My dad stomped off and it took everything in me not to kick the side of my tent. It wouldn't have been satisfying anyway, and it probably would have just fucked up the poles holding it up.

"He's having a hard time," my mom said in apology after my dad was far enough away. "This lockdown is hard on them. All the shit with the Russians, trying to figure out what to do, and then Heather shows up, a blast from the past. It's a lot."

"He's a dick," I replied, shaking my head. "I'm about done with the way he's treatin' her. That shit is seriously fucked up. She hasn't done shit to him."

"I know." Mom sighed. "I'll talk to him."

"Mick wasn't with her," I repeated, meeting her eyes. "They weren't like that."

"I never had any clue what was going on with them," my mom said with a shrug. "Put a shirt on, and you can walk with me."

"What, you can't stand the sight of your baby boy's manly chest?" I joked. I laughed as she swatted at me, then leaned into the tent and grabbed the last shirt out of my duffle. Hopefully Heather wasn't planning to light my dirty laundry on fire or anything, because she'd pretty much taken every piece of clothing I owned.

"I never knew what was happening with Micky," my mom said after we'd been walking for a little while. She'd steered us toward the back of the property until we were walking outside the perimeter of scorched grass. "He was so sweet and he always seemed so transparent, but damn that boy was quiet."

"Not with me," I said, smiling. "Little shit never shut up."

"Well, you were his best friend." She slid her arm through mine and laid her head on my shoulder. "I was his mom. Boys don't tell their moms anything."

"Nah, Heather was his best friend," I replied.

"Not true," she protested.

"It was true," I argued, still smiling. "I was cool with it. I was his brother. He could fart and scratch his balls when he was with me."

Mom laughed.

"But he talked to her about shit. Stuff he didn't want to talk to me about."

"Like what?" she asked, glancing up at me.

"How the hell would I know?" I joked uncomfortably. "I just said he was talking to *her*, not *me*."

"They were cute together," she said with a grin. "He was so much bigger. It was like a bear and a bunny becoming friends."

"Yeah. You remember the time out at the house when Mick kept tryin' to get Heather to stand on his shoulders?"

"I thought she was going to slap him," Mom said through her giggles.

"'Come on, Heather, just once, just so I know we can do it,'" I mimicked Mick's voice.

"'If you come near me I'm going to hurt you,'" Mom imitated Heather.

I laughed at her perfect impression. Heather had been so offended by the entire thing and that had made it even funnier at the time. I'd always kept my distance when they were hanging out, but we'd all been around her a lot that year when she and Mick were connected at the hip. I'd seen the way she'd looked at him… but more importantly, I'd seen the way he *wasn't* looking at her. He'd seen her as a friend, nothing more.

It was why I'd never tried to get in there. I wasn't all that fired up to play the Hawthorne consolation prize. It really didn't make any sense that I was screwing around with her now, but for the first time she wasn't looking at me like the asshole older brother of her best friend. No, when Heather looked at me it always felt like she was picturing my ass naked.

"I hope the guys figure out what the hell we're going to do," my mom said with a sigh. "This is the longest lockdown we've had in over twenty years. I'm about to go nuts."

"What, you don't like living in a commune?" I asked, wrapping my arm around her shoulders.

"I miss my house," she groaned as we headed back toward the clubhouse. "I want to be where the people *aren't*."

"Yeah, I hear ya," I said.

"How's your house coming?" she asked.

"Slow as hell." I laughed.

It wasn't common knowledge that I'd saved up and bought a condemned old house. The thing was unlivable and I didn't really want to hear about how it was a waste of money, so I'd kept the news to myself.

I'd always liked to build things. Fix them up. Make old things like new again. It's why I'd convinced Mick to pitch in on the 1972 Chevy Nova we'd bought when I was sixteen. He'd only been thirteen at the time, but between the two of us, we'd had enough cash to buy the old junker and slowly but surely we'd made her purr again. That was one of the benefits of helping out at a garage for years before you were actually legal to work. You got paid under the table, didn't have anywhere to spend the money, and learned mechanics early.

Now that the Nova was finished it was parked at my parents' house since I was usually on my bike, and I'd started a new project. The house was a disaster, no doubt, but that's what I dug about it. I'd gotten it for dirt cheap, and I was able to fix it up on my own slow schedule since I was usually sleeping at the clubhouse anyway. The place had rotting floorboards, no toilets, no electricity, broken out windows, and I had to check on it a couple times a week to keep homeless people from camping out, but it was mine.

It calmed me down better than anything else. Taking a sledgehammer to a wall not only seemed to mellow the rage I couldn't get rid of, but it was also productive. Left me feeling accomplished and shit. I was pretty sure that was one of the reasons my dad had helped me with the down payment.

"Do you have the electricity wired yet?" Mom asked as we reached the back door.

"Nah." I shook my head. "Gotta figure out where I want the walls first."

"One day, you're going to knock down a load-bearing wall and that entire place is going to fall down around you," she replied worriedly.

"I'm careful," I promised, stepping around my cousin Cam's twin boys who were building an elaborate Lincoln Log house in the middle of the hallway. "I know which walls to avoid."

"Callie, I'm gonna need you to talk me down," my Aunt Farrah called out as we passed the doorway to her room. "I'm about to strangle your brother."

My mom laughed. "I better go calm the nutjob."

She hugged my side, then spun around and walked into Casper's room. My aunt started yelling before she'd even closed the door behind her.

They were the funniest pair of friends I'd ever seen and they'd been friends for a long ass time. My mom was pretty mellow. She didn't get worked up about shit very often and when she did, my dad calmed her down quick. Aunt Farrah was the opposite. It was all drama with her, and my uncle Casper fucking encouraged it.

I walked through the crowded clubhouse and almost groaned in annoyance. There were people everywhere. You couldn't walk two feet without running into someone, and I completely understood my mom's cabin fever. I was lucky—I spent most of my time in the garage bays working and anyone who wasn't working wasn't allowed inside. It was too fucking dangerous to have the kids running around like little chickens with their heads cut off. When things were normal, it wasn't a big deal if someone brought their kid into work with them. Most of them were pretty well behaved and they were just stoked to be helping out their dad for the day. But when you got more than two together, especially during a lockdown? Chaos.

"Your dad still giving you shit?" my friend Leo asked as I bellied up to the bar.

I eyed the whiskey on the back shelf. "Is the world still spinnin'?"

"He'll mellow," Leo replied with a nod. I had a feeling that as a patched in member he knew a shit lot more than I did about what was happening with the club, especially since his dad was the president. "You with that blonde girl?" he asked, turning so he could lean back against the bar. "Hawk?"

"Why does everyone keep calling her Hawk?" I asked in confusion, turning to see what he was looking at.

Heather was sprawled out on one of the couches with Molly's daughter, looking at a little tablet. Whatever they were watching must have been playing music, because Rebel's head was nodding and Heather's bare feet were swaying where they hung over the arm of the couch.

"That's how she's been introducin' herself," Leo said, catching my attention again. "Hey, I'm Hawk, what's your name," he said with a snicker. "Bitch has said hello to damn near everyone."

That didn't surprise me. She'd never been one to sit quietly in the corner. The girl liked company.

"I've heard the little one call her that, too," Leo said, still staring at Heather. It was beginning to annoy me.

"Her name's Heather," I replied shortly.

His head turned slowly until he was facing me. "Think I'll call her

Hawk," he said with a smirk. He waited for me to say something, to lose my shit, but when I didn't, he got up and walked away.

I held my body still for as long as I could, then finally couldn't stop myself from turning to see where he went. He hadn't even gone near Heather, thank Christ. I could deal with Leo's bullshit when I knew he was poking at me; he was my best friend and I'd been dealing with his shit since birth. But I wasn't sure I could keep myself calm if I saw him with her.

★ ★ ★

"Got news," Dragon announced.

It was hot as fuck inside with the fans off and the doors closed, but it was the only place all of us fit if we wanted to have a meeting away from the women and kids. The officers had been holed up nearly all day in church going over shit I had no clue about. Apparently they'd decided to let the masses know something, because the minute they'd come out we'd been herded into the garage like cattle.

"Been waiting on the Feds to finish their little Russian round up," Dragon said with a smile. "Might as well let somebody else do some of the heavy lifting first."

Some of the guys chuckled, but most of us just waited.

"Russians have been havin' a hard time of it these past three weeks. Lots of their boys been picked up. Not just their soldiers. Men in charge. We got Rock to thank for most a'that."

The crowd grumbled a little. It didn't sit well with any of us that we were using cops to clean up for us. None of us cared if an enemy was picked up, not unless it affected us, but we sure as fuck didn't want to be helping put them away. We took care of our own shit, or at least we had before. If people in our line of work started snitching, no one on the planet would fucking trust us. The Aces were walking a very fine line.

"Know none a'you like this shit. I'm not likin' it either," my dad said, making the crowd quiet. "But we'll still get ours. Got men in most of the pens, if we don't we got allies who do. We'll take care a'business inside. Haven't given the Feds any news 'cept a list of names Rock had at his wedding. Nobody's testifyin'. Nobody's snitchin'… at least on our end. Can't say what those Russians are doin'."

"What now?" Homer asked.

"The Russian's are limpin'," Casper replied. He looked at my dad then back at the crowd. "Can't say that they'll be backin' off. We gotta keep our eyes up and our backs covered. But I don't see any indication that they'll be messin' with us in the near future. They're scramblin' to save their own asses."

My uncle was a genius. Not just smart, but a literal genius. He saw patterns where everyone else saw a mess of information that didn't make any sense. I was pretty sure he'd barely slept in the past few weeks as he'd tried to keep his finger on the pulse of what was happening outside our gates. Most of the officers had left at one point or another, meeting up with our contacts and gathering information, but Casper had stayed in the clubhouse. He'd locked himself inside the war room we called church and poured over the information everyone was bringing back.

They'd only given us the bare bones of what Casper had found, but I knew there was so much more they weren't sharing. It drove me fucking crazy, but there wasn't shit I could do about that. I wasn't even a patched in member yet. The fact that the other prospects and I were in the garage was a courtesy, nothing more.

"Lockdown's over," Dragon said with a sigh. "Thank Christ. But no big gatherings outside the gates." Everyone was silent as he let that sink in. "And you need to be on your women. They need to be keepin' their eyes open. Lettin' you know where they're at. You know the drill. And for fuck's sake, they make a new goddamn friend at the grocery store, you shut that shit down. These motherfuckers have tried over and over again to get us through our women and kids. That shit ends *now*."

We threw the garage doors back open, and I stepped outside with everyone else to get a breath of fresh air. The longer we'd been inside with it all closed up, the more it had felt like the walls were pushing in on us. It wasn't even a small space, but I'd been claustrophobic as fuck. Any discussion about the Russians made me jittery.

I grimaced as I walked toward a picnic table. When our barbecue had been shot up, we'd fought back. Well, the other men had fought back. I'd been tackled to the ground. I shook my head to dislodge the memory. They'd killed the men responsible. They'd even tracked down the fucker we'd thought planned the whole thing and had him brought back from where he'd hidden in Montana. We'd thought it was over. That they'd gotten all of them.

It wasn't until three weeks ago that we'd found out those fuckers were soldiers. Not planners. They hadn't been the brains, they'd just been taking orders from the fucking Russians.

I still didn't know how the officers had missed that when they'd interrogated the douchebag one of our allies had served to us on a silver platter, but I had a feeling I'd never know. Even after I patched in, I was pretty sure there was shit I was never going to be told.

My hands started to shake, so I got up and started pacing. Memories of the shooting seemed to come at me from all angles, and I was trying my damnedest to keep it all locked down. I couldn't lose it, not with the club still full of old ladies and little kids.

"You wanna go?" my older brother asked, startling me as he came up beside me. I hadn't even noticed he was still outside. I'd just assumed he would've gone in to tell his woman the good news and start packing up their shit.

"Nah, I'm good," I said, shaking my head. I kept pacing, though. Back and forth.

"Come on, fucker," Will said, taking off his cut and setting it on the table. "You know I'm not leaving your ass like this."

"Said I was fine," I mumbled in irritation. I could get it together. I didn't have a choice. My mom was still inside and I knew how she got when I lost my shit. It brought back everything for her.

"Just a friendly sparring match," Will said, pulling off his t-shirt. "You got me or Dad. No one else is comin' near you."

"Get the fuck outta here, Will—" I didn't even finish his name before his fist clipped me in the jaw.

"Fucker," I growled, barely staying on my feet.

Both my brothers had gotten their size from my dad. They were huge. I took after the other side of the family and was built more like my mom's brother Casper. I wasn't tiny by any means, but I wasn't built like a goddamn tank either. Any fight between me and Will was a joke. Even fighting with Mick had gotten my ass handed to me.

"Come on, baby brother," Will goaded. "Swing back, ya pussy."

I ripped off my cut and threw it on the table next to his, then acted like I was going to take off my shirt, too, but swung at him instead. My fist connected solidly with his jaw. He laughed at the sucker punch, but shook his head as if to clear it.

Then it was on. He was bigger, but I was faster and had a whole lot of rage to let loose. Even so, neither of us went full out. I wasn't out to hurt him, and he sure as hell wasn't there to hurt me. Big brother was giving me the outlet he knew I needed. And fuck, had I needed it.

We were sweaty, dirty as shit, and rolling around in the gravel when the crowd started to gather. I knew my dad would have kept my mom inside, so I ignored them. It wasn't the first time they'd seen a fight outside. It wasn't even the first time they'd seen us rolling around in the dirt.

Will had me in a headlock and I was punching him in the kidney when I heard her voice. Everyone was talking. It was loud as hell, but I still heard her above the others.

"Stop it! What the fuck! Someone stop him!"

Will's arm tightened around my neck, and my vision started to get spotty when I felt him jerk and then let me go completely. I dropped to the ground, landing on one arm, then was up again. And I couldn't fucking believe what I saw.

Will was kneeling, his chest heaving, and on his back was Heather. She had her arm around his neck, squeezing as hard as she could, and I was pretty sure she was trying to make him pass out. My brother's neck was thick as fuck with muscle. There was no way it would work, but she was still trying.

I met Will's eyes and he was smiling at me in amusement. He wasn't even trying to stop her. He'd just dropped his arms limply to his sides and was waiting for me to take care of it.

"Sugar, what're you doin'?" I asked as I pushed myself painfully to my feet. I was gonna feel that fight for the next week.

Heather didn't even look at me. She was so focused on what she was doing that she was completely oblivious to the fact Will had let me go.

"Heather," I murmured gently, touching her shoulder.

She let out a feral scream and jerked at the arm around my brother's neck before she realized who I was. Her breath was coming in short pants and I could barely see the blues of her eyes because her pupils were dilated so huge.

"Come here," I said softly, reaching for her. Before I could even grab her, she was off my brother's back and practically crawling up my body.

"He," she stuttered. She was shaking like crazy and her fingers gripped frantically at my ripped t-shirt. "He was—he."

"We were just messin' around, baby," I said, glancing around the crowd for her sister as she started to cry. "Come on, you've seen me sparrin' with Mick a bunch of times."

"That wasn't—" she stuttered.

I lifted her up until her legs were wrapped around my waist and felt her tears against my neck as we started moving away from everyone. We didn't need to give them a fucking show.

"Sorry, man," Leo called out quietly. "Tried to keep her back, but thought she was gonna hurt herself."

I ignored him as I reached up and pushed Heather's face deeper into my neck, winding my fingers into her short blonde hair. She could've gotten really hurt if we hadn't realized she was there in time. It was total fucking luck Will hadn't thrown her off as soon as he'd felt that arm around his neck. I wasn't sure how I would've reacted if she'd jumped on me.

"You gotta stop," I murmured as she kept crying, her body jerking with every hiccup.

"That was bad," she whispered back. "That was *horrible*."

"It wasn't," I argued calmly. I'd been headed toward my tent, but changed direction and moved toward the edge of the building. The tent was in the middle of everyone and I needed to get her alone.

"He was—" she stuttered to a stop again and sniffled.

"We were just messin' around," I said again, stopping once we were finally out of sight.

"That didn't look like messing around," she argued.

I let go of her so she would get down, but the girl had some serious muscle because she didn't even sag an inch down my body without my support.

I took a deep breath to try and calm myself down, but it wasn't happening.

"And you thought it was a good idea to get in the middle of that shit?" I yelled, startling the hell out of her. "What the fuck is wrong with you?"

That got her legs to drop to the ground and her arms to fall from around my neck.

"What?" she asked in confusion, tipping her head back to look at me.

"You have any idea what coulda happened to you? Either one of us coulda knocked your fuckin' teeth out before we realized you were there."

"He was—," she swallowed harshly, her eyes starting to water again. "He was *choking* you."

I could see how bad she was freaking out. She was still crying. Still shaking.

But now I was shaking, too. My stomach was in knots.

If there was one thing on this earth that got to me more than anything else—one thing that made me go fucking crazy—it was someone putting themselves in danger to try and save me. I couldn't handle that shit. Couldn't deal with it.

I reached out and gripped her face, leaning down so we were nose to nose. "Don't ever do that again," I ordered harshly. "You hear me?"

"I was trying to help you!" she yelled back, her voice cracking. "He was hurting you, I—"

"Listen to me!" I yelled back, making her flinch. "Don't you *ever* do that again."

"Okay," she whispered, tears rolling down her face and onto my hand. "Okay."

"Son?" my dad called, coming around the corner. "Everythin' good?"

"It's fine," I replied. I barely glanced at him because the minute he'd walked around the corner, Heather had put her hand over mine, and I couldn't tell if she was holding it against her face or getting ready to pull it away.

"Come on," Dad ordered. "Need to get everybody packed and get 'em the fuck outta here."

"I'll be there in a bit," I answered, watching Heather. She was still crying, but she wasn't making any noise. She wasn't even moving.

"Now, Thomas."

I looked at him in annoyance and noticed he'd moved a couple steps toward us. His entire body was braced and it took me a second to realize why.

He thought I was going to fucking hurt her. He thought he was going to have to step in.

Jesus Christ.

"Stop cryin'," I said, looking back at Heather. I couldn't deal with my dad then. *She* was the priority, not his fucked up view of me. "Come on, sugar. I can't leave ya like this."

"We can go home?" she asked, pulling my hand away from her face. "Finally." She sniffed and wiped off her face with the palms of her hands.

"Wait for me," I said, leaning forward to kiss her forehead. "I'll bring ya home."

She nodded but didn't say anything else as she slid past me and walked quickly toward the front of the building.

Two hours later when I went looking for her, she was gone.

Chapter 5

HEATHER

"Ahhh," I sighed as I dropped backward onto my clean sheets. I'd spent the last few hours cleaning the nastiness out of my fridge and wiping up the dust that seemed to have accumulated on every single surface of my house over the past three weeks. It was good to be home.

I'd kept up with my online summer classes while I'd been on the compound, but it was going to be so much easier doing homework from the comfort of my own bed. In the relative quiet of my own apartment. With my own orange soda in a glass on my bedside table. Wearing nothing but a sleep shirt and a pair of underwear. Bliss.

I was lucky. My parents had set up college funds for me and my sister when we were just babies, and since my sister hadn't used most of hers they'd added the leftover money to mine. The little windfall meant that I didn't have to get a job for the next four years. As long as I lived frugally I could focus solely on schoolwork. It drove my sister Mel crazy, but it wasn't my fault she'd dropped out of college, and my parents wouldn't let her use the money to backpack in Europe for a year.

It was kind of ironic, really. My parents went on at least two trips a year and they'd been to every continent at least once. They loved to travel and they'd passed on that love to my older sister. They just hadn't been willing to pay for Melanie to do it. As far as they were concerned, they'd earned the right and she hadn't. They'd pretty much always been that way. As often as they'd gone abroad, one would think Mel and I would've been stamping our passports from the cradle, but we hadn't. We'd gone on five family trips throughout my entire childhood and none of them had been outside of the United States. Instead, our parents left us with my aunt and uncle and their demon son while they saw the world.

I shuddered as I thought of my cousin Devin. The kid had terrorized me relentlessly until Mel was old enough for us to stay at home alone while our parents were gone. It hadn't mattered how often I told the adults what he was doing, they'd always brushed it off with a "boys will be boys" comment until eventually I stopped saying anything. I knew they'd begun to see me as a tattletale. It was almost as if the more I told them what was happening, the less importance they gave the offense, until it finally didn't matter to them at all.

My parents hadn't wanted to know. My aunt and uncle were the only ones that would keep us so they could go on their trips, and they hadn't been willing to rock the boat. Only Mel had understood how bad it was. She'd been the only one trying to stop it until Micky had come along.

When Mick had found out how Devin used to beat on me, I thought he was going to kill him. He hadn't. But a few days after I'd told Mick about the torture, my parents had gone to visit Devin in the hospital. He'd been admitted with a broken jaw, a broken arm, and a whole bunch of smaller injuries. Apparently, he told the police he'd been jumped, but he couldn't remember any faces or how many boys had done it. He'd also claimed he had no idea why it had happened. The little liar.

When I'd seen Will with his arm around Tommy's throat earlier that day, I could almost *feel* it. I knew the sensation of someone cutting off your oxygen. The way the muscles in their arm tightened until the pressure was so bad you thought you'd die before they let you go.

Pushing and pulling at them, but nothing made them loosen their grip. The way your vision went sort of grey at the sides, and sometimes you'd see little black dots right before everything went dark.

I hadn't even been fully aware of what I was doing as I'd pulled away from the guy who tried to hold me back. I'd had complete tunnel vision. I'd needed to get Will off Tommy, so I'd done the only thing I'd known how to do. The very thing that terrified me.

I'D WRAPPED MY arm around Will's throat and pressed as hard as I could against the vein on the side of his neck.

Thankfully, it had done what I'd intended—which was make Will let go of his brother—and I hadn't actually hurt him. Because whatever I'd been doing hadn't worked. Will had just knelt there while I squeezed. He hadn't been fazed at all.

I dug my fingers into my tired eyes as I remembered how pissed Tommy had been that I'd stepped in. His reaction hadn't been normal. I could understand him not wanting me to get hurt, but he'd been shaking when he was yelling at me. It hadn't been just anger that made him go off; there had been fear and guilt there, too. By the time his dad came over and ordered him away from me, I'd been so confused. Oh, Grease had acted like he needed Tommy to help with very important things, but we'd all known what the guy was doing. He was trying to separate me and Tommy… but I couldn't understand why.

Tommy was yelling, sure. But if Grease thought for one second he'd ever do anything to hurt me, he didn't know his son very well. Tommy and Mick were two of the most protective guys I'd ever met. I hadn't seen that side of Tommy much when we'd been younger, but I *had* seen it. Mick was usually around to make sure no one messed with me, but Tommy had been around to make sure none of the other girls were messed with either. He'd been a complete dog, there was no doubt about that. He'd screwed every girl in his class. But I saw him at almost every party we'd been to that year, and I wasn't sure, but I was pretty confident that most of the girls he "took home" he'd actually taken *home*. To their houses. So that some douchebag couldn't take advantage of them when they were drunk.

I hopped off my bed when there was a knock on my door, but I paused before swinging it open like I normally would. I wasn't expecting anyone. My shithole apartment didn't have a peephole, and the chain lock was so flimsy it was a joke.

Staying at the Aces' compound for so long had made me paranoid.

But maybe a little paranoia was a good thing?

I wasn't sure.

"Heather, open up!" a familiar voice called through the door. "I can pick the lock in about two seconds if you don't… or climb in that open slider on your back deck. Your choice."

I stomped my foot and it felt fantastic, so I stomped it again. Sometimes it was nice to throw a fit when no one was watching.

Then I opened the door.

"What are you doing here?" I asked in exasperation. I'd just taken off my pants and I sure as hell wasn't putting them back on just because Tommy had decided to visit my apartment for the first time ever. I was finally in my own space, dammit. He was harshing my mellow.

"Told you to wait for me and I'd take ya home," he replied, pushing past me.

I slammed the door closed and sighed dramatically.

"I didn't need a ride. My sister and Rocky dropped me off," I explained as I dropped back down on my bed. "How did you even know where I live?"

My apartment was tiny, but it worked for me. It had a galley kitchen, the smallest bathroom on the planet, and enough space for my king-sized bed, my dresser and some bookshelves. I didn't really need any more space than that. When I'd lived at my parents' house I'd spent most of my time in my room anyway. At least this place had a kitchen.

"Jesus, it's small," Tommy mumbled looking around the room.

"That's what she said," I said under my breath.

"Not to me," he replied with a wide smile.

I snorted.

Then we were both laughing.

"Seriously," I said as our chuckles died down. "What are you doing here?"

"You were pretty worked up earlier," he replied with a shrug. "Wanted to make sure you were good."

"I'm fine." I rolled my eyes. "Just a temporary case of insanity."

"It have anythin' to do with that kid me and Mick beat the shit out of back in the day?" he asked, stepping toward me.

"What?"

"You know—that kid that was messin' with you. It have somethin' to do with him?"

"Wait," I muttered. "You were there, too?"

" 'Course I was," he scoffed. "Someone had to drive."

"Oh," I said faintly, watching as he came even closer.

"Mick said he used to beat on you?"

"That was private," I replied, getting to my feet.

"Had to tell me somethin' when he asked me to help him."

"He should have lied."

"Nah, baby brother couldn't lie for shit," he said with a small smile.

Then his face fell as we both realized the lie for what it was. Mick had been very good at keeping secrets. One secret in particular.

"Well, thank you, I guess. I never knew Mick had help."

"Didn't want you to know," he said quietly, reaching out to pull on the hair lying against my cheekbone. Then his entire demeanor changed. "You got any food in here? I'm starvin'."

"No, I don't have any food," I groaned, dropping back down to the bed. "Everything was rotten. My house smelled like your tent when I got home."

"Ha. Very funny. Let's go get some groceries then."

"What?" I asked in confusion. Jesus, I couldn't keep up with him.

"Groceries. Food."

"But then I'd have to put on pants," I whined.

"God forbid," he said, grinning as his eyes slid down my body.

"Eyes up here, turbo." I gestured at my face.

"Come on," he said, walking toward the door. "Throw some pants on so we can go get some food."

"I'm not hungry," I argued.

"I am."

"So?"

"Feed me."

"Not my problem," I sang.

"Fine." He strode back to the bed. "We'll work up an appetite, then we'll go get food."

"I'm up!" I yelped, hopping to my feet. I rounded the bed and threw on a pair of jeans while he chuckled his way back to the front door.

"Shut that slider, too," he ordered. "You got a piece a'wood to put in the track?"

"A what?" I asked as I slid the door closed and locked it.

"A piece a'wood or something to brace the door."

"No," I said, drawing the word out. "I just use this nifty little locking mechanism right here."

"Swear to God, you've got a death wish. Come on, let's go."

"Why do you keep saying that?" I huffed as I grabbed my purse on the counter and stomped toward the door. "And how the hell are we going to bring back groceries on your bike?"

"Takin' your car," he replied as we walked out onto the landing.

"I'm driving."

"Of course you are," I mumbled as I locked the door behind us.

★ ★ ★

A COUPLE HOURS later, Tommy was still at my house.

We'd gone grocery shopping, then to the hardware store, then he'd helped me put away all the food and put a wooden dowel on the track of my sliding glass door so it wouldn't open, then I'd made us dinner and he'd helped me clean up afterward… and he was still there. Sitting on my bed. Talking about some condemned house he'd bought.

I was willing to admit that he wasn't quite the asshole I'd thought he was, but I still didn't understand what he was doing in my apartment. We'd never been friends. Sure, we'd almost gotten down and it had been great, but hadn't that just been a proximity thing? You're here, I'm here, we're both going a little stir crazy…

"You're not listenin' to a word I'm sayin'," Tommy said, laughing. "What the fuck?"

"I'm listening!" I protested. "Your house doesn't have electricity or toilets."

"Right. And when was it built?" he asked doubtfully.

"In the…" I paused waiting for him to fill in the blank. He didn't. "I don't know!"

"Jesus."

"Well!" I threw up my arms. "I'm trying to figure out what you're doing here! I haven't seen you in years, and then all of a sudden you're all up in my business, sitting on my bed and taking me grocery shopping and shit."

"You don't want me here?" he asked, rising to his feet.

"I didn't say that. But this whole thing is whack!"

"Whack?"

"That's what I said!"

He chuckled.

"What?" I grumbled.

"So last night you slept in my bed, this morning you were grindin' your ass against my dick, and tonight you don't want anythin' to do with me?"

"You're here for sex?" I asked.

"I'm here gettin' to know ya," he explained in exasperation. "What about this are you not understandin'?"

"I mean," my words trailed off as I glanced around the room for something to save me. "You barely talked to me when we were younger! Hell, you barely talked to me during the lockdown and now all of a sudden you want to get to know me?"

"Isn't that how it happens?" he asked. "You see someone you think is hot, you talk to 'em, get to know 'em, see if they're as hot in bed as they are outside it?"

"That's a stunningly accurate description of dating, yes," I grimaced. "But we already knew each other."

"Not in any way that mattered," he retorted, rubbing at the back of his head.

"You were a complete asshole to me less than a week ago," I pointed out.

"You hit me in the balls!"

"And you deserved it!" I jabbed a finger at his chest.

"If I deserved it, why'd you file off those vampire nails you had?"

"Because they were growing out and I couldn't get them fixed," I mumbled in embarrassment. We both knew that was a lie. I'd been too mortified to keep them after all the comments about them on the night of the fire. A couple of guys had mentioned them when we were outside, but even more of them had been making jokes once I'd gone inside. Usually, I'd ignore shit like that, but since I'd been stuck behind the gates with those idiots, I'd filed the points down that night even though I freaking loved them.

"Thought you were hot in high school," Tommy said. My eyes widened. "You're hotter now."

"I thought you wouldn't have let me anywhere near your dick in high school," I replied, echoing his words as I crossed my arms over my chest.

"I wouldn't have," he said, letting out a dark chuckle. "You were too busy moonin' over my baby brother."

"We were friends."

"Yeah, I been tellin' that same shit to everyone who asks," he growled, shaking his head.

"Okay, so?"

"So, you mighta been friends but that ain't what you wanted."

"Yes, it was," I argued.

"Yeah, okay," Tommy said, looking away. "I'm gonna head out. Thanks for dinner."

He walked toward the door and I wanted to scream in frustration.

"What the hell is wrong now?" I asked, throwing my arms up. "You're *leaving*?"

"Nothin's wrong," he assured me as I reached him. He slid his feet into his boots then lifted his hand and placed it on the back of my head. "Been a long day. I'm gonna head back and get some shut eye." He kissed me on the forehead and then he was out the door.

The man was going to give me whiplash! First he was all flirty and then he was bossy and then flirty again and then sort of lost in his own world and then flirty yet again. He couldn't seem to keep one mood or conversation for more than a few minutes, and then he was off on some tangent.

I shook my head as I locked the door. I didn't really have time to try and figure out Tommy Hawthorne's moods. I liked him and he was probably fantastic in bed, but I had other shit to keep me occupied. If he showed up again, then he showed up again. If not? Well, I'd lived without him for the first nineteen years of my life and I seemed to be doing just fine.

Shoving my pants down my hips, I shimmied a little so they'd drop to the floor, then left them where they were as I skip-hopped and jumped onto my bed. I rolled around a little until I was under the covers and let out a heavy breath. I had a full night of snore-free sleep in my future and I didn't plan to waste a single minute.

Well, maybe I'd waste a few minutes… I closed my eyes and I was back in that blue and gray tent with Tommy's solid body tucked in close to mine. I'm pretty sure I said his name when I came. Then I laughed at myself. I was such a loser.

Chapter 6
Thomas

I hadn't seen Heather for almost a week, and the shittiest part about that fact? I'd been counting the damn days. We'd been hella busy at the shop and I'd been working twelve-hour shifts every single day. The money was good because I was getting a ton of shit finished and out the door, but by the time I was done at night I was fucking exhausted and hadn't had the energy to stop by her place.

I was going to change that tonight. It didn't matter how many hours I worked. I needed to get the fuck off the Aces' property for a bit.

I was really hoping she'd let me in the door. I knew I'd been an asshole the last time I'd seen her, but she'd seriously pissed me off. I'd seen the way she used to look at Micky. She could tell me they were friends until she was blue in the face, but we both knew that she'd had a massive thing for him. It drove me nuts she wouldn't just admit to it and let it go. Then *I* could fucking let it go.

I didn't understand why she pretended she hadn't been in love with the kid. It might have been puppy love of the teenage variety, but she'd been head over heels for my brother. I hated that. I hated that she'd looked at him like that and she wouldn't even own up to it.

But what was even worse? The fact that I'd known she loved him, and after he'd died I'd never once checked up on her. I didn't think my parents had either. I wasn't even sure who'd told her he was gone.

After the shooting, we'd been dealing with our own mess. Mom had been in the hospital with a gaping hole in her chest from first a bullet and then surgery, Will had been laid up, too, with a couple bullet holes of his own, Rosie had been pretty much inconsolable, and I'd lost my fucking mind. My dad was the only one who'd held it together and I was pretty sure that had been a close thing.

We hadn't had time for Micky's little girlfriend. It was understandable, but I felt like shit about that now. While I'd been slowly losing my shit, who'd been taking care of Heather? Her sister? I liked Mel, but she didn't really seem the type. Molly was like a surrogate sister to Heather but I was pretty sure she hadn't even known about the connection between Heather and our family until recently, so it couldn't have been her.

Shit, she hadn't even been invited to the funeral. We'd had a quiet thing after Mom was out of the hospital and only close family had gone to it.

"Hey, TomTom, you just gonna stand there or are ya gonna get some work done?" my uncle called out from across the garage. He smiled cheerfully as I flipped him off, then he wiped his face, leaving a streak of grease across his cheek. I laughed and shook my head.

Casper didn't usually work in the garage unless he was doing maintenance on his bike, which was what had him there today. He was more of a numbers guy. He took care of all the books, legal and not-so-legal. It wasn't that he couldn't work as a mechanic. Shit, he knew more about engines than most of us put together, but he just didn't have time for it. Thank God. When he actually was in the garage he spent most of his time heckling all of the mechanics.

I grabbed the wrench I'd been looking for before I zoned out and dropped down to the creeper, rolling myself back under the car I was working on. Only a couple more hours and then I'd be done with the piece of shit.

★ ★ ★

"You're back!" Heather said cheerfully, opening her door wide.

Shit, did the woman ever wear pants? She was standing in the open door with nothing on but a men's thin white t-shirt and a pair of underwear with… yeah, that was the Zelda Triforce printed on the front.

"You ever wear clothes?" I asked as I ushered her backwards, closing the door firmly behind me.

"I'm wearing clothes," she argued, spinning on her heel and moving toward the kitchen area as I toed off my boots. "My house is a no-pants zone, though."

She got busy in the kitchen doing God knows what, and I couldn't help the grin that pulled at my lips. "Link is my homeboy" was written across the ass of her underwear.

"You're a Zelda fan?" I asked as I quietly unbuttoned my jeans and slid them down my hips.

"Isn't everyone?" She snorted. "I mean, I'm a huge Mario fan, too, but the Zelda merch is so much better so I—what the hell are you doing?" she squeaked.

"What are *you* doing?"

"*I'm* making dinner. Where are your pants?"

"This is a no-pants zone," I replied seriously. "Wouldn't want to break the rules."

"Right, because you're such a rule follower?"

"I'm a fuckin' Boy Scout." I nodded as I walked toward her slowly.

"Always prepared, huh?" she asked with a small smile.

"Well, not at the moment. But if I walk back to my jeans, I've got my supplies in the pocket." I kept a straight face, but when she burst out laughing I couldn't hold back my smile.

"You're such a dork," she giggled, spinning back toward the sink. "And I'm pretty sure you've got some of your supplies…handy."

"True," I murmured as I came up behind her.

She was so short that my dick was level with the small of her back, but that didn't stop her from arching and pressing her ass into my thighs as I slid an arm around her waist.

"Whatcha makin'?" I asked, using my chin to move her hair out of the way so I could kiss her neck.

"Just mac and cheese." She giggled as I bit down softly. "You want some?"

"If you feel like sharin'."

"Sure. Grab some bowls, would you?"

I gave her one last kiss and moved away to get some bowls out of her cupboard. None of her shit matched and most of it was chipped, but she'd seemed almost proud of that fact when I'd brought it up to her the last time I was there.

"You wanna eat on the bed?" she asked after she'd covered her mac and cheese with pepper.

"Is there anywhere else to sit?" I asked jokingly.

"The floor," she pointed out flatly.

"Bed it is. Hey, you got any ketchup?"

Heather froze on her way to the bed and slowly turned her head to look at me. "You did not just say that."

"What?"

"If you put ketchup on that mac and cheese, not only will your mouth be nowhere near me tonight, but I'll also toss your ass out of my apartment."

I waited for her to laugh, but she didn't. "Are you serious?"

"As a heart attack."

"You just covered your shit in pepper!"

"Pepper is acceptable. You want some pepper? I left it on the counter." She started for the bed again as I watched her in shock.

"I'm serious, Tommy. That's nasty," she said as she sat down and scooted back until she was leaning against the headboard.

"You're fuckin' crazy," I mumbled, following her to the bed. I didn't even want the mac and cheese if I couldn't have ketchup on it, but now it looked like I'd have to choke it down plain. Fucking disgusting.

"So how's life at the compound? Anything fun happen since I've been gone?" she asked before stuffing a huge bite into her mouth.

"You're gonna choke," I muttered, taking a small bite. "And, nah. Same shit, different day. Been working my ass off, though."

"Money, money, money," she sang, smiling.

"Yeah, it's nice. I've been tired as hell but I'm making bank."

"And what will you do with your windfall?"

"Is it called a windfall if you had to work for it?" I asked, shaking my head. "Any extra money's goin' into the house. Gotta get the wiring finished so I can start working on the floors and walls."

"Ah the house that was built in…" her words trailed off and she lifted her eyebrows at me expectantly.

"Nineteen fifty-two, smartass," I mumbled taking another tiny bite of the mac and cheese. "You woulda known that if you'd been payin' attention."

"Sorry," she grumbled. "In my defense, it was kind of hard to concentrate when you just showed up at my door out of nowhere."

"I'd just seen you that day!"

"Well, yeah," she replied slowly. "But that was another world, right? I mean, we were stuck there. It's not like we had a lot of choices for hookups."

My stomach churned. "You sayin' you don't want me here? You got some other guy?"

"No." She rolled her eyes. "If I didn't want you here I wouldn't have answered the stupid door. Don't get your panties in a twist."

I clenched my teeth against the urge to say shit that *would* get me kicked out of her apartment.

"Oh, come on, Tommy," she said in exasperation, setting her bowl on the table and reaching for mine so she could set it down, too. "I just didn't know that this was a thing, okay?" She crawled across the bed, and I leaned back a little as she straddled my thighs.

"You didn't answer the question," I growled, grabbing her wrists as she reached for me.

"What question?"

"You got another guy?"

"No." The word was drawn out in annoyance. "But if I did, he wouldn't be such a pain in my ass."

I let go of her hands and grabbed the sides of her face before the last word had even left her mouth. God, she was hot. Even when she was being a bitch she was sexy. Especially then.

She sighed when my mouth met hers, and her hands went to the sides of my neck as she sucked my bottom lip between her teeth and bit down. She tasted like pepper, but it wasn't bad. And her skin was so fucking soft. I'd known from before that it was, but my memory hadn't done it justice.

I slid my hands down her neck, carefully making sure I wasn't putting on too much pressure until I'd reached the wide neck of her t-shirt. Her collarbone felt tiny under my fingertips, but I forgot about how breakable she seemed as my hands finally reached her tits. She may have been small pretty much everywhere, but her tits were perfect. Round and firm with nipples that pointed slightly upward on a slope.

"Shirt off," she mumbled against my mouth before pulling away. "Off."

She lifted her hands above her head, and I grinned as I ripped the t-shirt off of her.

"Damn," I groaned as I leaned toward her breasts. I took one nipple between my lips and sucked it up against the roof of my mouth, making her whimper. I knew I was pulling on it kind of hard, but she'd seemed to like it hard when I'd gotten my hands on her in the tent, and she sure as hell wasn't complaining. Her hands wrapped around the back of my head and her hips rolled against me.

I lifted my mouth and jerked her hips toward mine, and we both groaned as she rolled her pussy against my cock. Holy hell. She was so short that I'd have to bend in half to get my mouth on her tits again from this angle, but I made good use of my hands as she continued to rock against me.

Her eyes were half closed and she was breathing heavily, but I didn't push for anything more. What she was doing would get me off before long, and I didn't want to break the spell. I knew that her little asshole cousin had beaten the hell out of her, but I wasn't sure what else he'd done and I wasn't going to make the big moves until I knew.

If she wanted more she'd have to tell me. Give me some type of signal.

I let out a startled moan when her hand slid down between us and underneath the waistband of my boxers. Her hand wrapped around my cock and squeezed.

I was pretty sure that was the signal. That was the signal, right? Oh, fuck, that felt good.

I pulled her hand away and threw my feet off the edge of the bed. Turning as I stood, I dropped her onto the mattress and shoved my boxers down my thighs.

"Me too," she said with a small grin, lifting her hips so I could pull off her underwear.

Then I just stood there. Like an idiot. Trying to take everything in at once. She was small, but she wasn't super skinny. None of her muscles were defined, but she had curves for days. Small waist, round hips, fantastic tits. Her pubic hair was trimmed short, but it was dark like her eyebrows and contrasted sharply with the blonde hair on her head.

"Nice dick," she finally said, making my gaze shoot up to meet hers. She smiled teasingly and I couldn't help but laugh in embarrassment. Yeah, I was staring.

Then I realized my condoms were across the room. Son of a bitch.

"Don't move," I ordered, glancing back down her body.

"I wasn't planning on it."

I nodded stupidly and practically ran to the front door where I'd dropped my jeans, fishing the condoms out of my front pocket as fast as I could.

When I got back to the edge of the bed, I found her curled up on her side with one arm under her head and the other covering her tits. She wasn't exactly hiding her body, but I knew with just one look that my fumbling had cooled things off for her.

"I'm fuckin' this up," I said softly, dropping the condoms on the comforter as I leaned over her. I ran my lips down her shoulder as I crawled onto the bed, and before I was even fully on top of her, she'd turned to face me.

"You're not fucking it up," she rasped, leaning up to kiss me.

"No?"

"No way." She raised her hands and ran them down my sides as her legs fell open, her knees bracketing my hips.

Her mouth dropped open as I slid down her body, running my open mouth over her chest. I pulled one nipple into my mouth and slid my tongue around it, then moved to the other one and gave it the same treatment.

I'd heard the guys talking about the taste of women, and I understood it. There was nothing like the taste of pussy. But when my mouth was on other parts of a woman's body, it was all about the texture for me. The softness of Heather's skin and the little ridges on her nipples made me insane. I fucking loved feeling the way her tits had a little give to them when I gripped them and the way her hip bones jutted out a little when she was lying on her back.

I moved my mouth down farther, running my tongue around the bottom curve of her breast before sliding it down the ladder of her ribs. Her stomach was smooth and just barely rounded, and she had a piercing in her belly button that I couldn't stop myself from pulling on a little with my lips.

"Tommy," she sighed as her fingers slid along the side of my face until one of her palms was resting just over my ear. I wanted to bite at her skin, rush so that I could finally feel her wrapped around my dick, but the way she cradled my face in her palm had me slowing down.

When I finally reached the nirvana between her legs, I groaned against her skin. The textures there were even better. The wiry short hair and the smooth slick skin were such a contrast that it made my head spin. Most of the women I'd been with were waxed completely bare. This was different. In some ways, it was hotter.

I slid my tongue over all that flesh and shuddered as the hair rasped over my tongue. Then I found her clit, already swollen and sticking out like an arrow pointing me to the promised land.

When I ran my tongue over it, she shuddered and her thighs tightened around my head. That was clearly what she needed. I moved my tongue the exact same way a second time, then a third, and soon her hips were thrusting against my mouth and she was whimpering and babbling shit I couldn't really hear with her thighs pressed over my ears.

I was hitting the right spot over and over, but after a couple minutes when she hadn't come, I knew she needed more. I loosened the grip I had on her thigh and smoothed my hand over her ass and between her legs. Damn, she was so wet, we were leaving a damp spot on the comforter. I groaned again when I slid my fingers inside her. She was clenched down so hard it was a tight fit. A really tight fit. Turning my hand, I curled my fingers upward and pressed gently. That was all it took to make her come, soaking my hand and the bottom of my face.

I let up on the pressure against her clit, but I left my fingers inside her as her cunt pulsed around them over and over. Yeah, I was gonna need to feel that against my cock at some point.

I finally lifted my head when her legs relaxed and fell back against the bed. She was lying there, gasping for breath, but I smiled when I saw that her hand was frantically searching the bed for the condoms I'd dropped.

"Come here," she ordered, curling her upper body toward me as I moved up the bed. I swiped my hand over my face right before her lips met mine, but the wetness didn't seem to bother her and she opened her mouth instantly so my tongue could slip inside.

"Damn," I groaned as one of her hands wrapped around my cock.

"Condom," she murmured against my mouth as she wrapped her legs around my hips. "Quick."

I lifted my head and searched for the packets I'd left on the bed, finally finding one stuck to her sweaty side. It only took me a minute to get it on, but it felt like an hour.

Then I was sliding inside. Slowly. Because even though she'd just come, she was tight as hell. I pulled back a little and tried again, but I only got a little farther inside. She was so fucking tight it was almost uncomfortable.

"Heather?" I asked quietly, lifting my head so I would meet her eyes.

She looked at me in confusion.

"You've done this before, right?" I asked, making her cheeks go red.

"Of course." Her words came out sort of shaky as I pressed harder against her.

"Don't lie to me," I warned, pulling out again, then pressing even harder.

"I have," she said, nodding her head as her fingernails scratched up my back.

I didn't believe her, but less than a second later I was bottoming out and I swear to God, my eyes rolled back in my head.

I pulled out again, then thrust back in, and slowly but surely her muscles loosened around me until the fit was tight but no longer felt impossible.

"That's so much better," she said on a sigh as her hands slid around to my chest, her palms flattening over my nipples.

I dropped down to my elbows and she moaned when my pubic bone met hers, giving her a little bit of extra friction against her clit. I wanted to get her off again, but I knew it wasn't going to happen. I could already feel my balls tightening as I thrust harder and harder.

My hands somehow got wound up in her short hair and I gripped it as my entire body started to shudder. I dropped my mouth back down to her neck and bit down as I came.

"We're sweaty," she said as my body relaxed on top of hers. She licked my shoulder. "Salty."

As I came back down from my orgasm, my mind finally cleared a bit and my head shot up.

"Were you a virgin?" I asked, pushing back up on my arms so I could see her face.

"I told you I wasn't!"

"Pussy says otherwise."

"I guess I should take that as a compliment, but it sure as fuck doesn't sound like one," she growled back, pushing at my shoulders.

I pulled out and fell to my side as she crossed her arms over her chest. I wasn't sure if she was trying to look tough or what, but the fact she was naked and spread out over the bed kind of ruined the effect.

"I could barely get in there," I mumbled, sitting up to pull the condom off. No blood. Thank God.

"So?" She hopped off the bed and pulled her shirt over her head.

"Why are you so goddamn defensive?"

"Because! I told you I wasn't and you kept asking. Why the hell would I lie?"

" 'Cause you didn't want me to stop?" I said confidently, getting to my feet so I could throw the condom away.

She snorted loudly behind me. "Please."

"Are we seriously fightin' right now?" I asked, turning to look at her.

"We wouldn't be if you'd stop being a jackass!" Her lips trembled and I felt like a dick.

"Doesn't matter if you were a virgin or not," I said, reaching out to pull her against my chest. " 'Cause you sure as hell aren't one now."

"I've had sex before," she said, wrapping her arms around my waist. "When I was fifteen."

"Oh yeah?"

She nodded against my chest. "Yeah. It sucked, so I didn't do it again."

I chuckled. "Usually does when you're that young."

"Not for the guy."

"True." I kissed the top of her head and pulled away. "Let's get you cleaned up."

I towed her into the bathroom and held her hand as I tossed the condom and turned on the shower. I wasn't sure how I'd fit inside by myself so I knew there was no way we'd both fit, but I led her inside anyway and left the door open so I could soap her up. I could tell she was a little embarrassed at first, but after a couple minutes she just stood there sleepily, letting me take care of her.

Twenty minutes later we were both clean and crawling back into her bed, underneath the sheets this time. Her house was pretty warm with no air conditioning, but her hair was still wet so I didn't open a window. It got pretty cold at night.

"Did you always want to be a mechanic, or did you just sort of fall into it?" she asked after a few minutes of quiet.

"Knew I always wanted to be an Ace," I replied quietly, pulling her tighter against my side. "Workin' in the garage goes hand in hand with that."

"If you could do anything else, what would you do?"

"Probably build houses. Restore 'em. I like fixin' shit up. Works out, though, I'm still doin' that now, just on my own time. Probably wouldn't like it so much if it was my job."

"Makes sense," she replied, drawing designs on my chest with her fingers. "Mick wanted to build race cars."

"I know," I said, smiling into the dark. My brother had loved anything fast—cars, boats, motorcycles, ATV's—it didn't matter what it was. "Probably coulda done it, too. Casper's always lookin' at ways to drum up new business."

"You think he would have joined the Aces?" she asked, her fingers pausing.

"Of course." I glanced down at her, but couldn't see anything but the top of her head against my shoulder. "Coulda done his own thing if he wanted, but I can't see him goin' far from family."

"I just—" She shrugged. "It doesn't seem like he'd fit in there."

"He would." I assured her, looking back at the ceiling. "We grew up with those people. They're family. Better than family."

She nodded but didn't say anything else.

"Why'd you tell people your name was Hawk?" I asked, remembering her walking around the clubhouse like she lived there. Mick wasn't the only one who didn't seem like he'd fit in there, but had.

"It's a cool name!" she said propping herself up on an elbow. "Everybody's got cool names. Dragon, Grease, Casper, Poet—that name is seriously fucking cool—uh, Hulk, Samson, Moose!"

"You're forgettin' some," I said, laughing at her excitement.

"Yeah, well, those are the coolest ones. You don't have one, though."

"Nah, not yet."

"Why not?"

"Lotta reasons. Haven't earned it. Poet's the one who doles those things out, gotta wait for the old geezer to knight you or some shit."

She giggled and dropped back down to the bed.

"I like him. He's from Ireland, huh?"

"Yep. Came over before his daughter Brenna was born. So did his wife, Amy."

"But her accent is different," she replied, her fingers once again sliding over my skin in indistinctive patterns. "She's not Brenna's mom, right?"

"Nope."

"There must be a story there."

"Yep."

"Well, are you going to tell me?" she asked, pinching my nipple.

I laughed as I pulled her fingers away from my skin and laced them with mine. "Alright, you ready?"

"Yes."

"You sure?"

"I'm going to hurt you."

I laughed again and squeezed her hand. "Alright, I'll give you the rundown."

"Wait!" She scrambled away from me and rolled off the bed, and I watched her bare ass jiggle as she slid the small window over the kitchen sink open. Then she was jogging back across the room and I got to watch other things jiggle. *Damn.* "Okay, now I'm ready," she announced as she curled back up against me.

"Alright, so Poet and Amy have been married since they were kids. But when they came over from Ireland, some bad shit happened, and they didn't get back together until like, twenty years ago."

"Whoa. And he had a kid with someone else even though they were still married?"

"She did, too."

"Really?"

"Yeah, that part's kinda cloudy though. Poet was livin' with Brenna's mom until she died, but I've never heard nothin' about Nix's dad."

"Nix? I didn't meet him."

"Nah, he's got his own shit. Lives up in Portland with his partner."

Heather stilled. "His partner?"

"Yup." I let that sink in. I was pretty sure she had a skewed idea in her head on how we felt about gay people. As in, we didn't give a shit what got people off, and for some reason she thought we did.

After a full minute of silence she spoke again. "Okay, how is everyone related to freaking everyone else?"

I laughed, making the entire bed shake. "Uh, okay so…"

"Out with it," she ordered.

"I am! Just trying to figure out how to explain it without confusin' ya."

"I'm pretty smart, I think I can keep up."

"All right. So, Poet was the VP of the Aces before my dad."

"Okay."

"Poet's daughter is Brenna. Brenna married Dragon who's our new President."

"This is supposed to be confusing?" she cut in.

"Shut it," I ordered, smiling. "Dragon and Brenna have two kids. Trix and Leo."

"Leo's the one with the scar?"

"Right. And Trix is married to my cousin Cam—you know him as Hulk."

"And they have those cute twin boys, right?"

"Yup. So that's their family."

"I'm following," she said firmly, though I knew she was probably going to have a hundred questions when I was done.

"Right. My mom and dad have Will, Me, Micky and Rose, you know that. Casper is my mom's brother, and he married her best friend Farrah."

"I like Farrah."

"Everyone likes Farrah," I replied. "You want to hear the rest or you done?"

"No, I want to hear it."

"Farrah and Casper adopted Cam when his parents died. Then they had Cecilia, Lily and Charlotte."

"That wasn't so confusing."

"Oh, and Farrah's dad was Slider, our old president."

"Jesus. You guys are like the Old Testament. Everybody marrying into the same family. Wait, *old* president? What happened to him?"

"Died," I replied, swallowing hard. "Same day as Mick."

"Oh," she said, so softly I felt it more than heard it.

"Story time is over," I announced, closing my eyes.

"Yeah, I got that," she murmured, kissing the side of my chest. "Goodnight."

" 'Night, sugar."

I took a deep breath and prayed to God I wouldn't have a nightmare that night. Twenty minutes later, I was still awake when Heather's quiet voice broke the silence.

"Was it you?" she asked. "Did you do it?"

"Did I do what?" I asked, stiffening.

"You know what."

I didn't move. Barely breathed. Of course I knew what she was talking about. I thought about it damn near every day…but I had zero remorse.

"Does it matter?" I finally asked.

She was quiet for a long time, so long that I didn't think she would answer me. Then finally, her lips met my chest again with a sweet kiss. "No. It doesn't matter."

Chapter 7
Heather

Oh, man. I smiled to myself before I opened my eyes. Sex was so much better than I'd remembered. I slid my arm out, but found nothing but cool sheets next to me, making my eyes pop open.

Where the heck was Tommy? I looked around the room, but he wasn't there. Then I realized how light it was in my bedroom and relaxed back against the sheets. He must have left for work hours before and I'd slept right through it.

I tossed back my covers and glanced down at my naked body, searching for evidence the night before. My entire body felt sore, but there weren't any visible marks. That was a little disappointing.

I hopped into the shower and got ready for the day with a smile on my face. I'd had a good time. The best time.

I'd dated plenty over the past couple of years, but I'd never had a guy sleep over. I was glad I hadn't protested when Tommy had shut off the lights and climbed back in bed with me the night before. I'd liked having him there. I'd even liked listening to his low voice explain his family tree. Talking quietly in the dark like that felt intimate. Too intimate, probably, which was why I'd asked him the question I'd promised myself I'd never bring up.

I grimaced as I got ready, remembering the way his body had tightened. He hadn't been expecting it. For the past two years, I'd never said a word, not even when we were talking every day at the clubhouse.

I probably shouldn't have said anything. No, I *knew* I shouldn't have said anything. Some things were best forgotten.

Suddenly, I was afraid he'd taken off the moment I was asleep. Had I pissed him off? He hadn't seemed angry, just wary, but maybe I'd read him wrong.

I shoved my feet into a pair of sandals and grabbed a banana off my counter. That's when I found the note he'd written on one of my school notebooks.

"Had to work. I'll see you after. Tommy." Then written even smaller at the bottom of the page, "You should bring me lunch."

I laughed and glanced at the clock. I had just enough time to grab some tacos from the truck down the street and head to the garage before lunch. Perfect.

★ ★ ★

"I'm here to see Tommy," I told the guy at the gate as I came to a stop.

"Pop the trunk," he ordered, making me roll my eyes.

"I was just here you know," I called out as he looked in the back of my car. "I was here for the lockdown."

"Doesn't matter," he called back as I pulled the lever to open my trunk. "Still gotta check it."

A couple minutes later I was moving slowly down the driveway to the garage, and I was sweating a little. Tommy told me to bring him lunch, so it wasn't like I was just dropping by his work, but I still felt weird. Grease didn't like me, and the guy was not only in charge but I knew he'd be at the garage. Maybe if I was lucky I could just slip in and give Tommy his tacos without anyone noticing I was there.

When I parked out front, I silently groaned. There were no less than ten guys standing around out front or sitting at the picnic tables in the grass. Son of a bitch.

"Hey, you forget somethin' here?" Rocky asked as I climbed out of the car.

"No, I—"

"She's here for Tommy," Leo called out, making me cringe.

"Oh, yeah?" Rocky said in surprise.

"I brought him tacos," I mumbled, shutting the door behind me, the bag of food clenched tightly in my fist. "Is he here?"

"Yeah, he's here," Rocky replied, nodding. "Yo, Tommy! Heather's here!" he called toward the garage.

"Your girlfriend's here," one of the guys at a picnic table sang.

"She brought you luuunch," someone else called.

The guys all laughed, and I grit my teeth in embarrassment. I could take a little ribbing. Usually I was the one *doing* the ribbing. But I barely knew those guys, and I was still waiting for Grease to come out at any moment and order me off the property.

"Hey, sugar," Tommy called as he came striding out of one of the big doors. "You bring me lunch?"

The guys heckled some more, but I barely noticed them. I was too busy staring at Tommy's smile as he crossed the pavement. He must have changed his clothes when he got to work that morning, because he was wearing a different set of work pants and a white tank-top that had seen better days. The sight made my mouth water.

"Hey," he said as he reached me, leaning down to kiss me softly. "Whatcha got in that bag?"

"Tacos," I replied hoarsely. Holy hell, I was turned on. I was turned on like I wasn't standing in the middle of a bunch of bikers who were watching us closely. *Shit.*

"Thanks, baby," he said, kissing me again. "You wanna eat out here or—"

"Not out here," I grumbled, making him laugh. "Are they still staring?"

Tommy lifted his head and looked around. "Yup. Come on, we can eat inside."

He took my hand and pulled me behind him as he strode past the guys who were still giving him shit. I followed him into the clubhouse and looked around in surprise at how different it seemed when there weren't a bunch of women and kids filling it up, then we were moving toward the back hallway and into the room I'd shared with the girls during the lockdown.

"This is your room?" I asked in surprise as he led me to the bed and sat down, pulling me between his knees.

"Not officially," he replied, running his hands up and down the outside of my thighs. "But yeah, it's where I sleep most of the time."

"Why not 'officially'?" I asked, trying to focus on anything but the way his fingers were sliding under my shorts with each pass.

"Not patched in. Only members get their own rooms."

"Wait, you're not an Ace?" I asked in confusion, glancing at the leather vest draped across the end of the bed.

"Nah." He reached out and flipped the vest over, pointing to one of the patches. "Prospect, see?"

"Oh, so does that mean that you're not actually a member or that—"

"You really want a lesson on club rules right now?" he asked, putting his hand back on my thigh.

"No," I whispered as his fingers pressed further under my shorts.

"Didn't think so," he whispered back, pulling on my legs so I'd straddle him. "Thank you for bringing me lunch," he said, leaning up to kiss me.

I ground my hips down against him, then froze. "We can't do this here," I said glancing back at the closed door.

"Why the fuck not?"

"Because they'll hear us," I muttered, my eyes wide.

"They'll hear us kissin'?" he laughed. "Leo's got some crazy good hearin' but I'm pretty sure even he couldn't hear that."

"No, but—"

"Oh, you're hopin' for more than that," he teased, stuffing his hands up the back of my shorts until he was squeezing my bare ass cheeks.

"Shut up," I gasped, smacking his shoulder.

"Come on, baby. Just the tip," he teased some more, laughing at the disgruntled look on my face. "Just a little, I'll pull out."

"Oh my God, you're annoying," I said, trying to climb off his lap. "See if I share my tacos with you."

My mouth shut with an audible clack as I realized what I'd just said.

Then he was roaring with laughter and tossing me onto the bed.

"Come on," he said, pulling my shorts off easily with one tug as I giggled. "Share your taco with me."

"Knock it off," I yelled, laughing.

"I'm hungry, woman," he growled back, tickling my sides. "Gimme a taco."

"You're such a dumb ass," I choked out, scrambling to get away from him. I rolled over to my belly then screeched as his hand connected with my bare ass.

I looked over my shoulder to see him smiling broadly, the thin strap of my g-string gripped in his palm. "Don't you dare," I warned, right before he snapped it in half. "Dammit, Tommy!" I hissed, rolling to my back again. "I'm wearing white shorts!"

"You're not wearin' anything now," he countered smugly, pulling my underwear away from my body.

I huffed in annoyance as he leaned down to kiss me, but I let his lips meet mine. Then I reached up and twisted his nipples through his shirt.

"Ow," he yelled, smacking at my hands as he laughed. "That fuckin' hurt!"

He pinned my arms to my sides and nuzzled against my chest, making me freeze. Oh, shit.

"I won't return the favor," he mumbled as he moved farther down my body. His hands left my arms, and as soon as I was free I ran my hands over his messy hair. I tensed as he lifted my shirt, but relaxed again as his lips ran over my stomach, going lower and lower until his face was between my legs.

"Ah, lunch," he teased, making me laugh until his lips made contact again.

He ran his tongue all over me, dipping inside then dragging it up to my clit over and over again while I tried not to make any noise. It took less than a minute before I was coming, my back arched off the bed and my short nails digging into his scalp.

He rested his head against my thigh while I caught my breath and then kissed me one more time before rising to his feet. "You brought food?" he asked, like he hadn't just been going to town on my vagina.

"Tacos," I said, nodding. "Where are my shorts?"

He snickered as he picked up my white shorts off the floor and tossed them to me, not even bothering to see if I'd caught them before he was reaching for the bag of food.

"Damn, these are good," he mumbled around a huge bite as I pulled my shorts back on. "Where'd you get 'em?"

"Truck by my house," I answered distractedly. I was staring at the front of my shorts, and without the nude colored underwear on, I was *sure* I could see the shadow of my fucking pubic hair.

"You look fine," he assured me with a crooked grin.

"Yeah, until I go out in the sunshine!"

"I'll walk ahead of you."

I opened my mouth to bitch at him, but before I could say anything there was a knock on the door.

"Tommy, cops are here," someone called. "Lookin' for you."

Tommy made an irritated noise in the back of his throat and stuffed the rest of the taco into his mouth as he got to his feet.

"Why are the cops looking for you?" I asked in confusion as he picked up the bag of food and grabbed my hand.

"Who the fuck knows," he replied, giving me a swift peck on the lips. "Better go find out."

He didn't seem concerned, so I tried not to be either, but I wasn't stupid. If the police had come all the way onto Aces' property, they were there for a reason, and it wasn't good. I followed him outside and forgot all about my see-through shorts as I got a good look at the patrol car parked sideways in the lot.

"You lookin' for me?" Tommy asked, squeezing my hand before letting go completely. He handed me the bag of tacos and walked toward the officers slowly, his arms loose at his sides.

"Thomas Hawthorne?"

"Yep."

"We need you to come down to the station and answer a couple questions for us," one of the officers said.

"What's this about?" Tommy asked calmly, looking back and forth between the two policemen.

"The disappearance of Mark Phillips," the officer replied.

It took every single ounce of reserve I had not to make any type of noise. I didn't fidget. I barely breathed.

"The teacher at the high school?" Tommy asked, seemingly confused.

"We can get into it down at the station," the officer answered.

Tommy nodded, then looked at his dad. "Make sure Heather gets home alright?" he asked.

Grease nodded.

Then, just like that, they were checking Tommy for weapons and putting him into the back of the squad car. He didn't even glance my way as they turned around and drove sedately back down the long driveway.

And I was frozen in place, my heart pounding in my ears.

"Heather!" Grease snapped, waving his hand in front of my face.

"Yeah?" I asked dazedly, turning to look at him.

"You got any idea what that was about?" he asked, glaring at me.

I stared at his angry brown eyes and swallowed hard. "None whatsoever," I finally replied, my voice solid and strong. "Do you?"

He didn't answer the question. Instead he stomped over to my car and opened the driver's side door. "Get in," he ordered. "I'll follow you home."

"You don't have to—" I said as I hurried to my car.

"Told my son I'd make sure you got home," he said, cutting me off. Then he walked away without another word.

I got in my car and started it up before backing slowly out of my parking spot. From the outside, I knew that I looked completely calm as I waited for Grease to pull up behind me on his motorcycle. I took off slowly and drove the speed limit the entire way home, then waved a little when I pulled into my parking lot and Grease continued past.

I walked coolly toward my front door, fit my key into the lock and let myself inside, shutting the door behind me.

Then my hands began to shake and I completely lost my shit.

★ ★ ★

"WHERE THE HELL is he?" I muttered to the universe later that night. I'd tried to do anything I could to keep myself busy. I'd finished my homework for the entire week, cleaned my apartment from top to bottom, washed and dried all of my laundry, and had finally dropped to the edge of my freshly made bed and bit my nails down so far one of them had started bleeding. I hadn't heard a word from anyone all day.

When my phone rang, I sprang off the bed and grabbed it, answering without even checking who it was.

"Hello?"

"Hey, sisterbeast," my sister's best friend Molly said quietly.

"Hey, Moll," I replied, reaching up to rub at my forehead where a massive headache was forming. "What's up?"

"I know it's kind of late, but I was wondering if Reb could come hang with you for a little bit?" She went quiet for a moment and then sighed. "Will's family is having some sort of meeting tonight and he wants me to go with him."

My eyes watered a little and I dropped the phone down at my side so I could clear my throat without her hearing. I raised it to my ear again when I knew I could speak without giving myself away. "Sure," I replied easily, sitting back down on my bed. "You sure you don't want me to come there?"

I held my breath as I waited for her answer. Rebel had Down Syndrome and was on the autism spectrum, so routines were a really big deal around their house. So even though I was waiting for Tommy to show up, I still had to make sure that having her over to my house wouldn't set her off.

"No," Molly answered. "Will would rather you weren't out driving by yourself this late. We can just drop her off if that's okay?"

"Yeah, no problem."

"Okay, we're leaving now. See you in ten."

When she hung up I tossed my phone on the bed and scratched my hands through my hair in frustration. The Hawthorne meeting had to be about Tommy, but I still had no fucking clue what was going on. Had he been arrested? Oh, God.

Vomit burned at the back of my throat, and I raced to the bathroom but by the time I got there, the feeling had passed. "Stop," I whispered, turning on the sink to splash water on my face. "Stop freaking yourself out." I braced my hands on the counter and counted backward from a hundred. Then I did it again.

By the time Molly was knocking on my door, I'd mellowed enough that I didn't look like a crazy person when I opened it.

"Hey, Sparrow," I greeted Rebel, reaching for her before Molly and Will had even stepped inside. "You gonna hang out with me for a bit?"

Rebel didn't answer, just laid her head down on my shoulder and sighed.

"She wasn't happy we were leaving the house, but she calmed down about halfway here," Molly said ruefully, setting Reb's bag down at the foot of my bed.

"Eh, it's all good," I assured her, rubbing Rebel's back. "We'll climb into bed and watch some Elmo for a while."

"Okay." Molly glanced at Will. "We shouldn't be gone very long, right?"

"Couple hours, max," Will replied with a nod. He looked at me. "You and Tommy, huh?"

"Um," I mumbled.

"You have any idea what the fuck's going on?"

"Language, Will," Molly chastised with a grimace.

"I was there when the cops came today," I said softly, rocking Rebel from side to side. "They said it had something to do with Mr. Phillips."

Will looked at me in confusion for a moment, then his expression cleared. "The teacher?"

"Yeah. He went missing a couple years ago."

"I remember that," Molly said in surprise.

"Anyway," I said. "That's what they told Tommy it was about."

"What the fuck would Tommy have to do with any of that?" Will scoffed.

"I don't know," I lied.

"We'll know more once we get to your parents' house," Molly said, putting her hand gently on Will's back. "We should probably get over there."

"Yeah," Will muttered. He turned and walked toward the door, then waited for Molly to come give Rebel a kiss and say goodbye before ushering her out of the apartment.

"Just you and me, kiddo," I said as I locked the door behind them. "Want to watch Elmo?"

A silent nod gave me my answer.

★ ★ ★

AN HOUR AND a half later I woke up to knocking on my front door. Rebel had fallen asleep, which was a huge deal considering she didn't have all of her sleeping stuff with her, and I'd fallen asleep shortly after. I'd been strung so tightly all day that by the time I'd gotten cozy with Reb, I'd been completely wiped.

"Who is it?" I called quietly before I disengaged the lock.

"Good answer," Will's deep voice called back through the door, making me smile.

"Hey," I whispered as I opened the door wide and let them inside. "She fell asleep."

"Seriously?" Molly asked, her eyes widening.

"Yep. My bed is magic."

Will snorted as he passed me.

"Everything okay?" I asked Molly as Will picked Rebel up and tucked her against his chest.

"Yeah." Molly glanced at Will then gave me an uncomfortable smile.

Well wasn't that some shit. I'd guessed Molly's loyalty had shifted, but I hadn't seen it in action until that moment.

"Save your questions," Will said as he grabbed Reb's bag off my kitchen counter. "If I know my brother, he's less than ten minutes behind us."

My heart thumped hard at that news and I smiled just a little.

"Thanks again," Molly said as she followed Will to the door.

"No worries."

As I closed the door behind them, I took a deep breath. Then another. Then another. I reached up and locked the deadbolt, but I couldn't force myself away from the door. I just stood there. Waiting.

Chapter 8

TOMMY

"How well did you know Mark Phillips?"

"Was he your teacher?"

"How often did you see Mr. Phillips?"

"What can you tell me about the altercation you had with Mr. Phillips in the high school parking lot?"

"Have you ever been to Mr. Phillips' house?"

"Have you ever been in Mr. Phillips' car?"

"Did you ever spend time with Mr. Phillips outside of school?"

The questions had felt never-ending. I was pretty sure that had been the point. You keep someone long enough and they'll answer you just to make you stop asking them the same thing over and over. Their answers will change to better fit your questions. They'll give you what you're looking for eventually.

Unfortunately for those detectives, they'd been dealing with me and not some kid who'd break down and cry for his mama. I'd answered their questions and no matter how they'd phrased them, I hadn't changed my answers.

"How well did you know Mr. Phillips?"

Not well. He was a teacher at my school.

"Were you and Mr. Phillips friends?"

No, he was a teacher. I just saw him around school.

"Did the two of you talk often?"

No, I didn't have any classes with him.

"Was he your teacher?"

No.

They'd tried to catch me in a lie, but they hadn't been able to and eventually had to let me go.

"Why the hell would they be askin' you about that missin' teacher?" my dad asked, leaning forward to brace his elbows on the table.

"No idea," I said, shaking my head. "I guess some kid thought they saw me fightin' with him or somethin' outside the school."

"Did you?"

"Hell, I don't remember. If I did it was probably about somethin' stupid like getting all of Mick's old essays from him."

"I asked you to get those," my mom said, reaching out to squeeze my bicep. "Remember? I had you go into the school and get all of his stuff."

"Yeah, Ma," I nodded, guilt for bringing her into it making me nauseous. I hadn't remembered she'd asked me to pick up Micky's stuff. I'd just remembered that it had been a pain in the ass. I hadn't wanted to talk to anyone and I'd gotten stopped in the halls fifteen times by people who wanted to tell me how sorry they were. I hadn't given a fuck how they felt.

"So that teacher just up and disappeared?" my dad said, watching me closely.

"The news said he just got in his car and drove away," I replied, holding eye contact. "No one has seen him since."

Dad glanced at Mom, then took a deep breath. "Okay," he said finally.

I'd asked my dad to pick me up from the police station when they'd finally let me go, and by the time we'd gotten back to my parents' house Will and Molly were already there waiting for us. Dad and Will were worried for good reason.

Getting picked up for random bullshit was standard in our line of work, but getting picked up for something completely unrelated to the Aces was pretty rare, at least for the guys who hadn't been evading warrants before they'd joined the club. On top of that, our lawyer had died the month before and we hadn't found anyone to replace him yet. Letting anyone who wasn't a member know our secrets—even the small secrets—was a gamble. We couldn't just pick anyone, so at the moment I would be stuck with some fucked up court appointed attorney if I was charged with something.

My dad's hair was getting grayer by the day, and it sucked that on top of dealing with the Russians he was going to have to deal with my shit, too. Even if I kept him out of it, he'd still be in it. That's how my family was. That's how the Aces were. They had your back no matter what.

"I'm gonna head out," I said, leaning over to kiss my mom on her temple.

"Didn't bring your bike over," my dad said, getting to his feet when I did.

"I'll take the Nova," I replied, pulling my keys out of my pocket. "Haven't taken her out in a while anyway."

Dad walked me to the door and pulled me into a hug before I could step outside. "You need me, I'm here. Alright?"

"Yeah," I answered, nodding. "I'll see you tomorrow."

"Sleep in," he called as I hopped down the front steps. "You've had a long day."

I couldn't tell if he was being sarcastic or not, but since he was technically one of my bosses, I decided I was going to take him up on the offer. I was headed straight to Heather's apartment, and I had no idea what I'd find when I got there. She'd either be at the door waiting to beat the hell out of me or fuck me blind, but either way I wouldn't be sleeping any time soon.

★ ★ ★

Heather opened the door before I could even knock.

"You couldn't have called?" she hissed. "Seriously?"

"Sugar," I started, before she cut me off.

"Don't say 'sugar' in that tone," she warned, walking away before spinning to face me again. *"What the fuck, Tommy?"*

"I handled it," I said, closing the door behind me and toeing off my boots. "It's fine."

"It's not fine!" she replied, her voice high and squeaky. "The cops picked you up! They were all, 'Do you know Mark Phillips?' and you were all, 'The teacher?' and they were all, 'Come with us' and then you were gone!"

"Calm down," I said quietly, walking toward her. "I took care of it."

"How? Seriously? Because I can't figure out why they would even ask you about him? I mean, *I can*, but weren't you careful?"

"Quiet," I ordered, pressing my hand over her mouth as I crowded her against the kitchen counter. I leaned down and spoke softly into her ear. "You know your neighbors? You know how thin these walls are?"

She sucked in a harsh breath and then nodded her head, reaching up to pull my hand away from her mouth.

"You're okay?" she asked, pulling my head away so she could search my face. "Everything's okay?"

"It's fine," I said again, running my hand through her hair. "I'm just fuckin' exhausted."

"I bet," she murmured, leaning forward to press her head against my chest. "I was worried."

"Nothin' to worry about," I soothed, wrapping my arms around her. "I'll take care of it."

I led her to the bed, shutting the lights off as we crossed the room, then stripped down and joined her underneath the blankets.

"You were careful, right?" she whispered as soon as we were comfortable. "They won't find anything?"

"They got nothin'," I murmured back, running my fingers down her spine. "It's a cold case. They'll give it up quick."

"And they won't ever find him," she said so softly that I barely heard her.

"And they won't ever find him," I confirmed.

"It still doesn't matter," she said as she kissed my chest, reminding me of the night before. I hadn't confirmed anything, but she'd guessed, and she'd known for sure the minute the cops had picked me up earlier.

The panic I expected to feel never came, but I lay there awake for a long time after she'd fallen asleep. If I'd learned one thing growing up on the Aces compound, it was the more people outside the club that knew your secrets the less likely they were to stay that way. I'd planned on taking my secrets to the grave, but I hadn't counted on reconnecting with Heather, the only other person on the planet who would see the connection between me and Mark Phillips.

She was the weak link. No matter how I looked at it, she was the only thing that could get me locked up. I could keep my shit together, no problem. I'd been dealing with cops and learning how to answer questions since I was old enough to talk. Heather wasn't like that. She panicked. Worried. Was intimidated as fuck by the police.

I ran it over and over in my head that night. How I'd keep her safe. How I'd calm her fears. How I'd keep the police away from her.

Only one answer made any sense.

I fell asleep with my brother's face smiling at me behind my eyelids and I woke up twice, gasping for breath with the echo of Micky's voice ringing in my ears. Thankfully, Heather slept right through it.

★ ★ ★

"MARRY ME," I said the minute she opened her eyes the next morning.

I was already up and dressed by the time she woke up and she looked at me in confusion for a long time before making a dismissive noise in her throat and stuffing her head back in the pillow.

"Hear me out," I said quietly, reaching out to rest my hand on her hip.

"I don't talk to crazy people this early in the morning," she mumbled back.

"As my wife, you're protected," I said, squeezing her hip. "The Aces watch out for you. Always. No matter what happens to me."

"I don't need protection," she replied, leaning up on one elbow. "What are you talking about?"

"If for some reason I get locked up—"

"You said everything was fine," she hissed, sitting up. "You told me last night that—"

"Heather!" I interrupted roughly, making her freeze. "Once we're married, you can't testify."

"What?"

"If we're married, they can't make you testify."

"I don't know anything," she said quickly, her eyes widening. "Why would they ask me anything? I don't know anything."

I leaned forward and kissed her, smoothing my hands up and down her arms until I felt the tension in her body fall away.

"You know enough," I whispered, pulling back to meet her eyes. "You know about Mick. Only a matter of time until they find that connection—if they haven't already."

"You think they'll come to me? Wouldn't they go to your parents first?"

"Even if they do, my parents don't know anything," I said, swallowing hard. "I was hopin' they'd never know."

"But your dad could help," she argued. "The Aces, they could help, right?"

"Maybe," I conceded. "But it might never come to that."

"But if you think that, then why all this marriage stuff?" she asked shaking her head.

"Sugar, they saw you with me yesterday," I reminded her, pushing her hair out of her face. "Probably know who you are by now. They start askin' around they'll know you were best friends with Mick. They start lookin' into Mick? Bingo."

"But married?" she asked, searching my face. "That's crazy."

"Was up half the night thinkin' about it," I said, sighing. "Can't think of any other way to keep you outta it."

"But they might not even talk to me," she protested. "You're making plans for something that might not ever happen."

Her phone rang and she reached for it, glancing at it before setting it back down. "Don't know the number, they can leave a message," she said dismissively.

"They start interrogating you and afterward we run off to get married, it'd look even worse," I said, glancing at her phone as it beeped with a voicemail notification. "We can get divorced later," I murmured. "If we can't stand each other, we can get it annulled or something."

"This is not how I imagined my first wedding proposal," she muttered, looking away.

I cringed.

"I'm going to have a cup of coffee and take a shower," she said with a sigh. "We'll talk more when I'm fully functional."

She climbed off the bed and shuffled to the kitchen while I lay back on the bed and stared at the ceiling. I felt like an asshole. She was nineteen. She didn't want to get fucking married. Hell, *I* didn't want to get married. I'd figured I'd have years before I found someone I wanted to make a family with, and when I did I'd do the whole proposal on one knee thing. It sounded like bullshit, but I knew that if I found the right woman, I'd want her to have a story she could tell her girls about. A story she could be proud of. Heather wasn't getting any of that.

She made a noise in the kitchen that had me shooting off the bed, and when I turned to face her she was white as a ghost.

"That was Detective Robertson," she said shakily, waving her phone in front of her. "He left a message asking me to call him back."

My hands grew clammy as I waited for her to say something else.

"Give me forty-five minutes," she said finally, setting her phone carefully on the counter. "Then we'll go get our marriage license."

She didn't look at me as she walked to the bathroom and closed the door quietly behind her. As soon as I heard the shower go on, I pulled out my phone and checked what the marriage laws were in Oregon.

Then I called my brother.

★ ★ ★

"That was easy," Heather commented as we climbed into the Nova a couple hours later. "You don't even have to do blood tests or anything."

"The next part is the hard part," I mumbled, turning the key.

We'd picked up our paperwork at the county clerk's office and the next step in our plan was to go tell my parents we were getting married. I'd suggested going to Heather's parents first to use them as a practice run, but she'd nixed that idea. Apparently they weren't very close so she was just going to call them instead.

"Do you think your dad's eyes will shoot lasers?" she joked wanly as she leaned her head back. "Because if you think he has lasers, I should probably just stay in the car."

"It'll be fine," I lied, tapping my fingers on the steering wheel. "My mom will keep him calm."

"Oh, God. I didn't even think about your mom," she grumbled.

"She'll be happy. She'll think you're pregnant—but she'll be cool."

"That's some fast work," Heather joked, looking pointedly at my junk.

"Just let me do the talking," I said firmly, reaching over to put my hand on her thigh. "It's nobody's business but ours. They can either be excited or not, it makes no difference."

"Maybe if we just told them—"

"No," I cut her off, squeezing her leg. "We want to get married. That's all they need to know."

"No one is going to believe it," she said nervously. "They'll think we're idiots."

"Why wouldn't they believe it?" I asked, giving her a small smile. "I'm clearly crazy about you."

"Of course you are," she said easily. "But that doesn't mean you'd ask me to marry you."

"I did ask you."

"Not because you're in love with me," she mumbled, turning her head to stare out the window.

Something in her tone made my chest tighten, and I jerked the wheel at the first driveway we came to, putting the Nova quickly into park.

"What are you doing?" she asked, looking around the empty parking lot.

"Hey," I called, unbuckling her seatbelt. "Come here."

"Let's just go, Tommy," she said, shaking her head.

"No, come here," I ordered again. I unbuckled my seatbelt and reached for her, yanking her onto my lap.

"What are you doing?"

"I'm crazy about you," I said seriously, running my hand up the back of her neck so I could grip her hair in my fingers. "No joke. I like you."

"I like you, too," she said pointedly, trying to scoot off my lap.

I ignored her movements and waited until her eyes met mine again. "All this shit wasn't happenin', we'd wait and see how it goes," I said softly. "But that's not how it played out. As long as we're together, though—I'll be good to you. I won't cheat. I won't ever lift a hand to you. I'll take care of you."

"I don't need you to take care of me."

"That's why I want to." I leaned forward and kissed her, barely brushing my lips against hers. "For as long as this lasts, we're a team. Okay?"

"Okay," she murmured, dropping her forehead against mine. "I'm kind of freaking out."

"Nothin' to freak out about," I promised her, wrapping an arm around her waist. "We're two idiots that are too young to get married but are doin' it anyway. End of story. People can say whatever they want. We're a team now. What they say don't matter."

"Let's go get this over with," she said with a sigh, reaching up to place her palm against the side of my face as she kissed me gently. "If your dad says any rude shit to me I'm gonna junk punch him."

I laughed as she climbed back into her seat. "That's probably not your best idea," I muttered as I pulled out of the parking lot.

It took us twenty minutes to get to my parents' house, but it felt like five. By the time we pulled in, Heather's knee was bouncing like a jackhammer and my palms were sweaty as fuck. I didn't know how other people did it—got married even though they knew their family was going to freak the fuck out. Maybe it was different when you were in love and sure you were doing the right thing. I was sure I was doing the right thing, the best thing, but I was still nervous as fuck when I climbed out of the Nova and met Heather at the front of the car.

"Let's do this," she said, giving me a goofy smile as she grabbed my hand.

She'd been visibly anxious the entire day, but it was as if all of a sudden she'd tucked that anxiety away and she was full of confidence. She didn't even falter when I ushered her inside the house and we found Molly and Will sitting in the living room with my parents. I hadn't wanted to worry her more by letting her know I'd asked my brother to meet us there, too, but I was hoping his presence would keep things relatively calm. I'd been sort of counting on Rebel being in the room so my dad couldn't lose it, but I didn't see her anywhere.

"Hey, guys!" my mom said in surprise, flashing us a wide smile. "Why the hell isn't anyone working today?"

"Dad told me to take the morning off," I said, leading Heather farther into the room. "We just wanted to drop by and give you guys some news."

My dad's eyes narrowed and he sat forward while my mom and Molly looked at us in confusion. Will settled back in his seat like he was waiting for the show to start.

"We're getting married," Heather blurted with a smile. She lifted up her hand and flashed the tiniest diamond I'd ever seen in my life. Thank God she'd had something to put on her finger before we'd left her apartment, because I hadn't even thought of it.

"You're what?" my mom asked dubiously.

"We're getting married," I answered, looking at my dad. "This Friday."

"Bullshit," my dad said. He didn't raise his voice, but Heather still stiffened at my side, her fingernails digging into my arm.

"We went and got our paperwork this mornin'," I told him calmly. "It's not bullshit."

"You're a child for fuck's sake."

"Legal in every state," I retorted flatly.

"You think I don't got enough on my plate?" he asked, rising to his feet.

"Asa," my mom murmured, following him up.

"I thought we were done dealin' with your bullshit," he muttered. "Why the fuck did I buy you that house?"

"You didn't buy my motherfuckin' house," I spat back, my skin heating with embarrassment. "You helped out with the down payment and I already fuckin' paid you back!"

"Jesus Christ," he muttered, scratching at his beard.

"We just came to let you know," I said stiffly. "That's it."

"You just came to let us know that you're marryin' some cunt you barely know, and—" His words came to an abrupt stop when my fist met his teeth.

"Thomas!" my mom yelled.

Before anything else could happen, Will was stepping between us, shoving my dad backward. "Get outta here, Tommy," he ordered. "Now."

I shook my head and glanced back at Heather, who was pale and visibly shaking. "Come on, sugar," I called softly, reaching out my hand.

Before I could take another breath, her fingers were clasped firmly in mine.

"I'm sorry, Ma," I said as I pulled Heather against my side. "I told you I wasn't gonna take anymore of that shit."

"I know, baby," Mom replied, her eyes filled with tears. "I'll talk to him, okay? And I'll help anyway you need it with the—" she stuttered to a stop. "With the wedding. If you want me to."

"I have no idea what I'm doing, so that would be awesome," Heather said with a small smile.

Then I was dragging her out of the house and down the front steps. When we climbed in the Nova she let out a shuddery breath and turned to look at me.

"The hard part's over, right?"

"Yeah," I muttered.

"How's your hand?"

"It hurts like a bitch," I said, shaking it out before stuffing the keys into the ignition.

"Jesus," she said. "You sure know how to make an announcement."

Chapter 9

Heather

"I'M GETTING MARRIED," I announced, pulling the phone away from my ear as my sister started yelling.

I'd known she would be the hardest person to convince I wasn't insane, so I'd saved her phone call for last. When I'd talked to my parents, they hadn't said much. They'd confirmed I'd still be attending college and that Tommy had a steady job and wouldn't be living off my college fund and they'd agreed to be at our wedding later in the week. It was as simple as that. My parents loved me, but they'd pretty much stopped 'parenting' when I'd been old enough to cook my own food.

It was Mel that I had to convince everything was great. She was the one who'd made sure I'd gotten to school on time. She was the person who'd held back my hair when I was sick and had helped me move into my apartment.

My parents may have loved me, but Mel was the one who'd always taken care of me.

"You're out of your mind," she finally said, her rant coming to an end. "You're not getting married for Christ's sake. Rocky got married when he was young. You know how that turned out."

"Well I'm not marrying a Russian mobster's daughter, so I think I'll be okay," I snapped back, exhausted by the day's events. Everything was happening so quickly that I hadn't had a minute to just sit by myself and let it all sink in.

"No, you're marrying into the *Aces*," she said incredulously.

"Oh, so it's fine for you but not for me?"

"You're better than I am," she blurted. "You have all this stuff going for you. You're in college. You're super smart and ambitious."

"That's stupid," I argued, my throat tight. "Don't say shit like that. Besides, I'm still going to go to school. I'll still get my degree."

"Yeah, until your new husband knocks you up."

"Oh, that's bullshit! Newsflash, Tommy and I are already fucking and it isn't 1952."

"I'm just saying," she retorted. "Priorities change when you get married."

"I'm not having kids any time soon," I said firmly. "I'm still going to get my degree."

Mel huffed and went silent. After about thirty seconds she finally spoke again. "Okay, what time on Friday?"

The rest of the day passed in a blur. Tommy and I didn't do much, mostly just hung around the apartment while he made calls, letting people know about the wedding. Dragon agreed we could have it in the field behind the clubhouse, and I found it incredibly ironic we'd be getting married right on top of the scorched grass where we'd first started talking again.

There wasn't a single person congratulating us without also trying to talk us out of it. As the day went on Tommy grew quieter and quieter, and by the time I started making dinner he was sitting silently on my patio staring out into the night.

He was trying to do the right thing, I knew that, but as his eyes grew darker with every phone call he made, I wondered if we were going about everything all wrong. Tommy was so adamant his parents could never find out about Mick, he was burning bridges left and right. I wasn't so sure that we couldn't have told them *something*. We could have explained our plan somehow while leaving Mick out of it, but every time I'd even mentioned letting Grease and Callie know what was really going on he'd shot me down.

"Hey," I said, standing in the doorway. "Do you want fajitas or baked chicken? I have the stuff for both so I—"

"Whatever you want," he replied, cutting me off.

I nodded even though he wasn't looking at me and walked back inside, anxiety making me nauseous. I'd agreed to his plan. I'd gone to the county clerk's office for the paperwork, tagged along to his parents' house even though I'd known it was going to be terrible, and I'd announced our news to my family. I'd done all that with the knowledge that Tommy and I were a team. That even though we weren't in love, and even though no one was supportive, we were going to stick together.

Suddenly, I was feeling very alone.

★ ★ ★

"Are you coming to bed?" I asked later that night.

I'd fallen asleep right after dinner, worn out from the day's events, but three hours later I'd woken up to find myself alone. Tommy was still sitting in a lawn chair on the back patio, the scent of pot wafting from him, and his head tipped up to the sky.

"What are you doin' up?" he asked as I stopped in the open doorway.

"I rolled over and you weren't there," I said, wrapping my arms around my waist.

"You sound like a wife," he joked, tapping his lighter on the edge of the chair.

"Don't," I said hoarsely. "Don't do that."

"Don't do what?" he asked lazily, rising to his feet and setting his pipe and lighter in the chair.

"Don't make jokes about it."

"Who was joking?" he asked, crowding me back into the apartment.

"I'm going back to bed," I announced. I hated his tone. The way his lips were pulled up in a sarcastic smile. The way he was looking at me. I hated all of it.

He was miserable. I could *see* it. But none of the bullshit we'd been through that day had been my idea.

I turned away, but before I'd taken two steps, his arms were wrapped around my waist and his face was pressed against the side of my neck. I froze.

"This is gonna all work out," he said, dropping one of his hands to run it lightly across my belly.

"Let's just go to bed," I murmured, refusing to relax against him. He was ready to kiss and make up after completely ignoring me all night? That was great. But I wasn't so ready to start getting cozy again.

For as many people as had told him he was an idiot, and nuts, and going to regret marrying me… just as many had called me a bitch and a cunt and pussy. As in, "You're really gonna throw your life away on some pussy?"

I'd talked to those people. I'd spent three weeks with them. I'd played with their kids. I'd helped the women make dinner and I'd played pool and horseshoes with the men. And not one, not a single one had said, "Oh, Heather? I liked her." I'd never given a fuck about people's opinions of me, but for the first time in my life I was experiencing the sensation of having a large group of people actively disliking me. I hated it.

It made me feel small.

"Come on, sugar," Tommy said with a sigh. "We'll deal with all this shit in the morning, yeah?"

I felt tears sting the back of my nose as he shuffled me across the room and gently helped me back into bed. It only took him a minute to strip down and then he was crawling in behind me and wrapping himself around me.

I fell asleep with his breath against the back of my neck, but I woke up to him yelling and shooting up off the bed like he was possessed.

"Tommy?" I asked, my gaze shooting around the apartment to try and figure out what had him jumping out of bed. "What's going on?"

He didn't answer me. His breath was coming in loud pants, and as I looked him over I noticed that not only was he covered in sweat, but the sheets were damp too. My clothes were clammy and stuck against my back.

"Are you sick?" I asked quietly, pushing back the covers.

He still hadn't answered me as I rounded the bed, but he jerked away when I laid my hand against his side. He wasn't hot. There was no way he had a fever when his skin was so cold and clammy.

"What's going on?" I asked as he bowed his head and wrapped his fingers around the back of his skull.

"Just a bad dream," he rasped out, shaking his head. "Just a fucked up dream."

"Come back to bed," I said softly, leaning down a little so I could peer up into his face. I was afraid to touch him again in case he pulled away. It had stung enough the first time.

"Gonna hop in the shower first," he replied. He took a couple of unsteady steps backward then spun and went into the bathroom, closing the door behind him while I stood there in confusion.

The shower turned on and I shook myself out of my stupor. He'd tell me what the dream was about if he wanted to. Asking him would just make him defensive. I knew at least that much about my future husband.

I stripped the bedding off the bed, and was almost finished remaking it when Tommy came out of the bathroom.

"Thought you'd be asleep," he mumbled. He was completely naked but didn't seem to care as he strode toward the bed.

"The sheets were kind of damp, so I put some clean ones on," I replied, throwing the last pillow back on the bed.

"Sorry about that," he said, finally meeting his eyes.

Just looking at him became painful then. It was as if every word he'd never said, and every hurt he'd ever felt were right there in his eyes, drowning him.

"Baby," I whispered, my own eyes tearing up.

I didn't move toward him, because suddenly he was right there, his hands in my hair and his mouth on mine. He groaned into my mouth when my hands came up to grip his sides, and one of his hands dropped straight down to push at my underwear.

"Need ya," he said against my lips, pushing me back onto the bed so he could strip my panties down my legs.

As soon as I was bare, his fingers were on me, petting and pinching and pushing until I was on the brink of orgasm.

"Slow down," I whispered, reaching up to cup his face in my palms. "Tommy."

He made a noise in his throat then raised his eyes to meet mine as he pushed inside me.

"You don't try to save me," he said, completely confusing me. "I take care of you."

"What?" I asked as he wrapped an arm under my ass and pushed me up the bed.

"Promise," he said, bracing his elbows on the mattress so we were locked together from chest to thighs. "If something happens, you take care of *you* first."

"What's going to happen?" I asked, my eyes watering. "Tommy?"

"Just promise," he murmured, dropping his forehead against mine. He wasn't even thrusting his hips anymore, he was just grinding, pressing, trying to get closer.

"I promise," I said, searching his eyes.

"You take care of you first," he ordered. "Say it."

"I'll take care of me first," I replied softly. I knew the instant I said it, and his eyelids drooped in relief, that it was a lie.

★ ★ ★

"Wake up, wife," Tommy said early the next morning, running his fingers up and down my bare back.

"I'm not your wife yet," I replied, throwing my arm over my head. "Go away."

"Can't. My mom's on her way over."

"What?" I screeched, pushing frantically up onto my knees and swaying for a minute as I tried to get my bearings.

"Calm down." He laughed as he reached out to steady me. "Told her you were sleepin' so you've got an hour."

"Why aren't you at work?" I asked, pushing my hair out of my face.

"Called in," he said as I got off the bed. "Gettin' married tomorrow, figured it was as good a reason as any."

"True," I said, stumbling over to my dresser for some clothes. "Why is your mom coming here?"

"Her and my Aunt Farrah are takin' you dress shoppin'," he said casually.

I froze.

No.

Hell no.

I spun slowly to face him. He was watching me closely, but without any expression on his face. "Say again," I said, narrowing my eyes.

"Pretty sure they called your sister, too," he replied, leaning forward to rest his elbows on his knees. "Not sure about your ma, though."

"Are you outta your fucking mind?" I asked dubiously.

"She called this mornin' askin' if you had a dress. What was I supposed to tell her?"

"You were supposed to say anything that didn't end up with me shopping for a wedding dress with your mother!" My voice rose with every word until I was practically yelling.

"What's the big deal?"

"This isn't a real wedding."

"Yes, it is."

"No. No, it's not."

"You gonna say vows to me?"

"Yes."

"You gonna mean 'em?"

I paused, thinking it over. Was I?

"Yes," I finally replied.

He got to his feet and stepped in front of me. "Then it's a wedding. You're marryin' me."

"But it's—"

"We're gonna try and make it work, right?"

"Yes." I sighed.

"Then you're gettin' a dress."

"What are you going to wear?" I asked, leaning against him as his hands started stroking up and down my neck.

"Want me to dress up?" he asked, a smile in his voice.

"No dirty t-shirts," I grumbled.

He laughed and I felt his lips against the top of my head. "I'll clean up."

"Leave the scruff on your face," I ordered, making him laugh again.

"Like that, do ya?"

"Especially between my legs," I replied, nodding.

He groaned and I smiled. "Jesus, go get ready. You've got forty minutes until we're overrun."

I ran to the bathroom and took the fastest shower ever, hissing every time Tommy yelled the countdown through the door. Thirty minutes! Twenty minutes! Ten minutes!

I was just sliding a summer dress with skull and crossbones all over it over my head when someone was knocking on the door.

"You ready?" Tommy asked.

"Yep." I threw the covers back up the bed so it looked somewhat made just as he opened the door, and women started pouring in.

Like, a bunch of women.

More than just Tommy's mom and aunt.

Callie and Farrah were there, but so were Brenna and Trix, Amy, Cecilia, my sister and Molly.

"Nice dress," my sister said with a roll of her eyes, making Tommy snicker.

"Hi Heather," Callie said, giving a little wave. She couldn't do much more than that considering the amount of people in my tiny ass apartment. I was pretty sure we were breaking fire code. "We told a couple of the girls," Callie told me with a small shrug. "Everything usually ends up being a group activity."

"Uh, okay," I mumbled, looking around the room.

"Do you know everyone?" Farrah asked, gesturing around.

"Yeah," I flashed a small smile. Oh, dear God. This was going to be bad.

"Okay, let's go then." Farrah looked over at Tommy. "You guys are gonna kill each other in the first month if this is all the space you have."

"We have a bed and a kitchen," Tommy replied with a smirk. "Don't need much more space than that."

Farrah laughed and shook her head while I felt my cheeks freezing in embarrassment. I refused to even look at Callie as she ushered all the women back outside.

"Have fun," Tommy said, snagging my wrist as I tried to follow them out the door.

"I'm going to hurt you," I hissed as he tugged me toward him.

"Just go with it," he ordered, kissing my unresponsive lips. "I'm gonna get some shit set up while you're gone."

"What shit?" I asked suspiciously.

"Chairs, music, kegs."

"Oh, for fuck's sake," I muttered, throwing my arms in the air.

What had started out as a quiet wedding was turning into a goddamn circus.

"It's fine," he said quietly. "The women'll deal with the food. You'll figure out flowers and a dress today. Easy."

"I'm not wearing a big poofy dress," I warned him, glaring as he smiled.

"Wear whatever the fuck you want," he said, dropping another kiss on my lips. "Now go."

I yelped as he smacked my ass as I was walking away, but I didn't even bother turning around, I just flipped him off over my shoulder.

★ ★ ★

"What are you looking for?" Brenna asked as I froze in front of a bridal shop. The display window was full of gowns, mermaid style, princess style, long and lacy, sleeves and strapless.

No.

"Not this," I said, immediately feeling like an asshole.

I knew they were just trying to be supportive, but the entire thing seemed fake. Just the day before, most of these women or their husbands had been on the phone with Tommy telling him what a bad idea getting married was. They'd cajoled and given out dire warnings and in some cases made me out to sound like a crazy bitch who was luring him in with my magic vagina. I'd *heard* them. My apartment was tiny. It had been impossible for Tommy to keep his conversations private. They'd said all those things, yet most of them had assumed that Tommy and I had been seeing each other before the lockdown. None of them had any idea that we'd gotten together only a couple of days before.

"Yeah," Farrah said with a nod, looking me over. "I get you."

She turned to the group of women who were getting out of their cars and standing on the sidewalk. "This isn't the place," she announced. "Follow me."

She tugged me back to her car where Callie was standing, talking to someone on the phone. "Let's go, Cal," she said as she threw open her door. "We're goin' somewhere else."

"What?" Callie asked as she stuffed the phone back in her purse. "Where are we going?"

I cringed and climbed into the back seat, keeping my mouth shut as Farrah explained to Callie that the bridal shop was too prissy.

"I'm sorry, Heather," Callie said, her embarrassment apparent.

"No," I said, my voice squeaky. "It was fine, I just—"

Farrah started laughing. "She doesn't want to look like a fuckin' cake topper."

Twenty minutes later we were pulling into a strip mall and parking in front of an antique store.

"Before you say anything, just trust me for a minute," Farrah said, meeting my eyes in the rear view mirror. "Afterward I'll take you for a surprise."

I snorted, but couldn't help but smile back when she grinned at me.

I liked Callie, but Farrah and I seemed to speak the same language.

Everyone was complaining and asking what the hell Farrah was doing as they climbed out of their cars, but Farrah ignored them. She just looked at Cecilia who was also smiling.

I followed her inside, past a bunch of different vendor stalls with everything from old Pokémon cards to china. Most of it looked like junk, but I kept my mouth shut. She'd said I should trust her, and I was curious to see what the surprise she'd promised was.

"Holy shit," I mumbled as Farrah came to a stop, throwing her arms out wide.

Hanging in front of her, surrounded by even more junk, was a gorgeous, off-white 1930s wedding dress. It had a deep v-neck, short flowing sleeves that looked like they'd hit right at my elbows and a short train.

"We found it a few months ago," Cecilia told me as I stared. "But my boobs would make it obscene and Mom wouldn't have anywhere to wear it. We almost bought it just in case Lily's boobs don't get any bigger." She laughed a little.

"Fucking gorgeous, right?" Farrah asked as I stepped inside the little booth and unhooked the hanger from the ladder it was hanging on. The dress was really well preserved. I couldn't find any holes or stains, and the back was just as gorgeous as the front.

"Will it fit?" Callie asked.

"If it doesn't, I can alter it," I whispered wide-eyed.

"You're welcome," Farrah said smugly.

"Damn, that's going to look fantastic on you," Trix said, nodding her head.

"Tommy better not wear a dirty t-shirt," I muttered as I looked back at the dress. I pulled the price tag away from the sleeve and almost swallowed my tongue.

"Don't look at that," Mel ordered, taking the dress out of my hands. "Oh, Jesus. Mom gave me literally ten times that much to pay for your wedding dress."

"She did?" I asked.

"Yeah, she's working today, but she wrote me a check."

"Oh."

"It's all good," Mel said with a smirk. "We'll find other uses for the money."

"Thatta girl," Brenna said, speaking up for the first time. "We still need flowers, manicures and pedicures, something for your hair—"

"A headband," Molly announced, cutting Brenna off. "That dress needs a blingy headband."

"Enough!" Farrah announced, raising her hands in the air. "I promised Hawk a surprise first."

Mel paid at the register as everyone else filed out of the store, but I couldn't make myself walk away from the dress. I knew things were getting out of control, and I felt my stomach churn, but I still couldn't look away from that gorgeous dress.

"It doesn't need to be wrapped up," Mel said quickly, when the employee reached for my dress with grimy hands. "Thanks, though!"

A couple minutes later we were flying down the freeway with my dress hanging in the seat next to me. I reached out to touch it and ran my fingers over the silky fabric. I was pretty sure it was real silk. My heart began to race.

Long white gowns weren't my thing. I wore pop culture t-shirts and tie dyed shorts. Doc Martens. My favorite dress had little anatomically correct hearts all over it. I swallowed hard and opened my eyes wide, trying not to cry. What the fuck was I doing?

"We're here," Farrah announced outside a brightly painted house.

"This is my surprise?" I asked, quickly following her out of the car.

"Trust me," she said again. I really wished she'd stop saying that, but I had to admit that her last surprise had been pretty epic.

I followed her up the porch steps and through the front door, and I couldn't help the wide grin that spread across my face.

"This is where you'll spend your mom's money," Farrah announced, her tone making clear exactly how she felt about my mom's absence. She nodded toward one of the display cases and I walked over to it slowly.

Inside was row after row of body jewelry. It wasn't the cheap stuff either. It was gold, and diamonds, and emeralds, and sapphires.

"Perfect," I whispered, catching sight of a delicate diamond stud shaped like a flower.

"Need help?" someone asked, walking out from behind a curtain where I could hear tattoo needles buzzing.

"Can I see that one?" I asked, pointing to the one I wanted.

"Sure. You looking for something for your nostril, too?" she asked, pulling out the little case. "This one has a coordinating ring."

She pulled out another case and pointed out the nostril ring. It was gold, too, and along the edge that would wrap around the outside of my nostril was a row of tiny diamonds.

"Oh, look," Trix joked, looking over my shoulder. "Those diamonds are the same size as your engagement ring."

"Shut it," I joked, lifting my eyes to the woman helping me. "I want those."

She named a price that was insane and I glanced at my sister.

"Whatever you want," Mel said. "Get 'em."

"Do you want to switch them out now?" the woman asked, reaching under the counter for my sterilized jewelry.

I bit my lip. There was no way I could change them out myself, but I kind of didn't want Tommy to see them until the wedding. It was stupid. It wasn't a real wedding, no matter what he said, but…

"I can switch them for you," Farrah called out from across the room where she was looking in another case. "If you want to wait."

"I'll wait," I said, glancing at my sister again to find her giving me a small smile.

The rest of the day was spent running all over town. We went to a flower stand and bought a shit ton of flowers, back to the bridal store that I'd balked at for a headband, to a salon for a touch-up on my blonde and to get my completely massacred nails done, and finally ended up back at Farrah's house where the women sat around her huge kitchen table picking through the flowers we'd bought.

"We didn't get a cake," I said as I sat back in my chair. "We can just get one from the grocery store right?"

I was halfway out of my chair before Callie spoke. "It's taken care of."

"It is?" I asked, dropping back into my seat.

"Yep. Don't worry."

"I wasn't worried," I answered automatically, making everyone laugh.

Oh, God. What was I doing? Somewhere along the line I'd gotten caught up in their planning and I'd forgotten reality. My stomach turned.

Chapter 10

Thomas

"Lookin' for your mom," my dad said abruptly the moment I answered my phone that afternoon. I was staring at the black button down and new pair of jeans I'd bought, hoping like hell I'd gotten the right thing. I hadn't bought anything but t-shirts, hoodies and work pants in years and I had a feeling I was going to look like a douchebag at my own wedding.

"She's with Heather and the girls," I told him, glancing at my boots by the front door. They were scuffed as hell, but I could probably get most of the dirt off of them. Heather was just going to have to deal.

"What?" my dad barked. "What girls?"

"Aunt Farrah, Cecilia, Brenna, Trix, her sister and Molly," I rattled off, grabbing the shirt off the bed to hang it up. I sure as shit wasn't ironing the thing, so hopefully keeping it hung up would work.

"What the fuck?" my dad bellowed, startling the shit out of me.

"What?"

"We were pretty fuckin' clear when we told everyone not to be havin' get togethers off club grounds," my dad said, making me freeze. "You know where they're at?"

"They were helpin' Heather out with wedding stuff."

"Of-fuckin'-course they are," he snapped, before breaking the connection.

Shit. Things had been pretty quiet for the last couple of days, but I knew there was shit I didn't know about going on behind the scenes. I had a feeling they were keeping even more from us prospects than usual. My dad knew something he wasn't telling me.

I dialed Heather and she picked up after just one ring.

"Where are you?" I asked, already sliding my boots back on.

"I'm at your aunt's house, doing flowers," she said dryly. "Where are you?"

Ah, shit. My hands shook as I locked the door behind me and jogged down the stairs outside. I fucking hated my uncle and aunt's house. Didn't like being there, and really didn't like Heather there.

"I'm on my way," I said as I climbed on my bike.

"What? Why?"

I didn't answer her, just ended the call and put my phone in my pocket.

When my dad and the guys got there all hell was going to break loose.

★ ★ ★

WHEN I PULLED up in front of my aunt's house, Casper and Dragon's bikes were already parked out front, but thankfully, my dad's wasn't. I walked up the stairs quickly and let myself in without knocking when I heard Dragon's raised voice coming from inside.

"...told you not to be havin' fuckin' hen parties when we're dealin' with this shit, Brenna!"

"No, you didn't!" she yelled back, making me cringe. She was the only person I'd ever heard talk to Dragon like that. Ever. In my life. "You told us not to have parties off club grounds! We went wedding shopping! We just got here and I was getting ready to call you!"

"You think they're gonna care where you're at?" he bellowed as I walked into the kitchen. They were staring at each other from across my aunt's dining room table and the women sitting at the table were caught in the fucking crossfire. "They don't give a shit if you're at the motherfuckin' nail salon! Someone sees a group of Aces old ladies rollin' around town with no protection, not even a goddamn prospect, what you think they're gonna do?"

"We were fine! We took separate cars and we kept our eyes open!"

"Jesus Christ," Dragon muttered, running his fingers through his hair. That's when I noticed the gray streaking through the black. He'd aged ten years in the last three.

Heather's wide eyes met mine from across the room. She looked freaked the fuck out and I couldn't blame her. Not only were people pissed as fuck about our wedding, but now the old ladies were getting into it with their husbands about it, too. I heard a bike out front and tilted my head, stepping farther into the kitchen when I recognized the pipes. My dad had shown up, and I was pretty sure Hulk had, too.

"Trix," Dragon said as I made my way around the table to Heather, stepping in behind her to rest my hands on her shoulders. "You're too old for me to beat your ass, but thank Christ I know your man'll do it for me."

"Shit," Trix muttered as she got to her feet. She must have heard Hulk's bike, too.

"Come on, baby," I murmured into Heather's ear, helping her up from the table. "We'll leave 'em to fight it out."

"What about Molly and Mel?" she asked quietly as Trix and Hulk started their own screaming match in the entryway.

"Guarantee their men are already on their way," I said, shaking my head.

I hadn't even thought to make sure the women had someone with them when they went out shopping. Brenna almost always had a shadow and so did my mom. It was so common there wasn't any reason for me to check on it. Hell, I'd played bodyguard more times than I could count.

I walked Heather to the front door and almost made it outside before my dad came stomping in. He was scowling and I felt Heather shrink into my side as he passed us, but he barely glanced our way as he followed the sound of Dragon's voice to the kitchen.

"Your dad hates me," Heather said as I led her outside.

"He doesn't hate you."

"Oh, yeah," she chuckled humorlessly. "He does."

"My dad's got a lot on his plate," I told her, pulling her toward my bike. "It's got nothin' to do with you."

"He thinks I'm just making my way through the Hawthorne boys," she said quietly as we came to a stop. "He's never going to let it go, is he?"

"Hey," I called, pressing under her chin with my fingertips so she'd look at me. "My dad's gonna calm down. I promise."

"What are we doing, Tommy?" she whispered. "I bought a wedding dress today. We got our nails done. I got a fucking tiara. What the *hell* are we doing?"

"Jitters," I murmured, pulling her against my chest. "It's just jitters."

"No, its not," she argued, her voice growing panicked. "We should tell your parents, at least. They should know what's going on. Even if the police never talk to me, they could still arrest you or something. What the hell would I do? What would I tell your parents? They should know, Tommy. They should—"

"Stop," I ordered, cutting into her freak out. "Everything is gonna be fine. I told you I'd take care of it."

"We're getting married tomorrow," she whispered frantically. *"Married."*

A couple more bikes came rolling down the driveway and I lifted my chin at my brother and Rocky as they rolled to a stop beside us.

"They kiddin' us with this shit?" my brother asked as he climbed off his bike. "Where were you?"

"I had shit to do today," I answered. "Thought Brenna had her shadow. Didn't even think to ask."

"Nah," Rocky said, walking toward us. "Kid's had the shits all day."

Just then something loud crashed inside the house.

"Aw, fuck. Someone's throwin' shit," my brother muttered as he passed us. "Aunt Farrah's gonna flip."

As soon as the two of them had gone inside, I got on my bike and jerked my head at Heather. "Climb on," I ordered, grabbing my helmet and stuffing it on her head. "We'll talk when we get home."

"I never even said you could move in," she said in frustration as she threw her leg over the seat. "We didn't even get that far."

"You wanna live in different places?" I asked, scoffing.

"Yeah, I'm sure that would convince everyone," she snapped sarcastically. "But we didn't even talk about it."

I shook my head and turned on my bike, drowning out whatever she said after that. I wanted to get the fuck out of there. Just being on my aunt and uncle's property made me twitchy. I didn't know how they'd continued living there after the shooting. Four of us had died in their back yard. Our entire world had been torn apart right outside their back door, but they hadn't moved. When my cousin Lily had been released from the hospital, they'd come right back home. It blew my mind.

I realized when we were halfway back to the apartment that it was the first time Heather had ever been on the back of my bike, which was kind of nuts. It highlighted the fact I'd known her for years, but I really didn't know that much about her. I wasn't sure what her favorite food was or what she was going to college for. I didn't even know her birthday.

I turned away from the apartment and felt her pinch my side, but there wasn't really any way to tell her where we were going until I'd parked in front of my house. I felt her scramble off the bike and looked up at the old beast, taking in the peeling paint and wrecked siding with a grimace. I hadn't taken anyone to the house except my parents when I'd first bought it, and I was pretty sure it looked worse than it had then.

"Is this your house?" Heather asked, walking toward the slanting porch.

"Stop!" I ordered as she got to the base of the stairs. I hurried toward her and put my hand on her hip. "Second step is almost rotted through, fourth one has a nail stickin' out," I warned.

She nodded and stepped gingerly around the spots I'd pointed out before stopping at the front door.

"Well?" she said, gesturing for me to go first. "Give me the tour."

I chuckled and unlocked the front door, pushing in ahead of her. I probably shouldn't have even bothered with locking up. It didn't keep anyone out of there if they were trying to get in, but I liked the feeling of unlocking the place. My place.

"Not much to show," I said with a grin, glancing around the bottom floor. Most of the walls were gone, and the few left up were half covered in peeling wallpaper.

"Whoa," she replied, slowly walking further into the house. "It's a lot bigger than it looks from the outside."

"That's 'cause all the walls are gone," I replied dryly, kicking some wood out of the way.

I grabbed her hand before she could walk into the kitchen and tugged her up the stairs to the second floor. The stairs were one of the first things I'd fixed when I'd gotten the place. I was always working by myself, and I really hadn't wanted to fall through the fucking stairs and get stuck there.

"So there were four bedrooms," I explained when we reached the second floor. "And one bathroom. But I tore out most of the walls—"

"I see that," she mumbled, looking around.

"And I was thinkin' that I'd make one big master with a connected bathroom, and then I'd frame in the other two bedrooms with a Jack-and-Jill bathroom between 'em."

"A Jack-and-Jill bathroom, huh?" she teased, moving across the floor.

"Just makes sense with the way the house is laid out," I replied, shrugging.

"What have you done since you got it?" she asked, looking out one of the few windows still intact.

"Fixed the stairs and the floor up here," I answered, stepping up behind her. "And tore down a bunch of shit."

"Are you going to sell it when you're done?" She leaned back against me.

"Don't know," I replied simply. "Figure it'll depend on where I'm at. If I've got a family. This is a pretty solid neighborhood. Big yard and shit."

"Well, I like it," she announced, spinning to face me. "I wanna help."

"Oh yeah?"

"Definitely. I'll help paint, and put in tile and all that stuff."

"So in about two years when I'm almost finished—that's when you want to help?" I laughed.

"That sounds about right," she said, nodding.

I smiled and kissed her. I couldn't help it. She was grinning happily, the stress from earlier completely gone, and she was so fucking pretty.

"Your mom was like a general today," she said as she pulled away.

Okay, the stress wasn't *completely* gone.

"She had a list of things for us to do."

"Yeah?" I asked, pulling away. "Did you get it all done?"

"Of course."

"You get a dress?"

"Do you think she would have let me leave if I hadn't?" she asked in frustration.

"You're gettin' worked up over nothin'," I told her, gesturing for her to head back downstairs. "We couldn't just sneak off and get married. You think my dad's pissed now? That shit woulda sent him over the edge."

"Maybe they're right," she mumbled, running her hand along the wall to keep herself steady on the stairs. I needed to get a railing in.

"Heather," I called as she walked toward the front door. My jaw was tight as she spun to face me, but I kept my voice calm. "You're either in this or you're not. I'm not forcin' ya to do anything. But I'm gettin' real sick of tryin' to fuckin' convince ya. I know you're savin' my ass, alright? If you wanna bail, you need to tell me now."

I knew I was asking a lot. Fuck, if not for me, she wouldn't be dealing with any of this bullshit. The police could ask her questions, she could answer them however she wanted, and it would be over for her. It was that simple.

Heather didn't owe me a goddamn thing.

"I'm in," she said softly, still standing by the front door. "I told you I was, and I am."

"I know my parents are makin' shit hard," I said, moving toward her. "But I'm a grown ass man. I own a house—a shitty house—but it's still a house. I work full time. Bought my car and bike myself. I love 'em, but they don't make decisions for me."

"We're a team, right?" she asked, tipping her head back as I got close. "Me and you."

"Me and you," I confirmed. "We're seein' how it goes just like we'd be doing anyway, considerin' how shit-hot the sex is." She giggled and I smiled. "We'll just have a piece a' paper that says no cops, or Aces for that matter, can come between us."

"Okay." She straightened her shoulders and nodded firmly. "We're doing this."

"I think we've got more goin' for us than most," I said quietly, reaching out to push her hair away from her face. "We know what this is. We're not goin' into it with stars in our eyes, expectin' everythin' to be perfect. It's protection, baby. Plain and simple. And men and women have been marryin' for that reason for thousands of years."

"You're right," she said, reaching out to squeeze my waist in a hug. "We know what this is."

We stood silent for a few minutes in the doorway of my house. Shit was gonna get complicated. I could feel it in my gut. We might have been getting married the next day, but that sure as fuck wasn't going to solve any problems.

The cops could still question Heather, and they would. She just wouldn't be forced to testify if anything went to court, which would help a hell of a lot. I didn't know what they had on me, but I was crossing my fingers it wasn't much. There was no way they'd found Mark Phillips, but I had no idea what they might've found in his house.

And all that shit was the least of my worries, because by the way my dad and Dragon had flipped out about the women that day, something far worse was going down.

"You ready to head home?" I asked Heather, smoothing my hand down her back until it rested at the top of her ass.

"Yeah," she replied. "I need to practice my makeup for tomorrow."

I let out a breath of relief and ushered her back to my bike. I was going to deal with one thing at a time. Tomorrow was the wedding. As long as we got through that, I'd deal with the other shit afterward.

★ ★ ★

"WE'RE GETTIN' MARRIED today," I whispered in Heather's ear the next morning, sliding my hand up her stomach and wrapping my hand around her tit.

"But not until later," she rasped, arching her back and rolling her hips against my cock.

We were already naked. We hadn't bothered putting anything on after we'd fooled around the night before, and as I reached down and ran my fingers through the little thatch of hair between her legs I found her already wet.

"Were you havin' a good dream?" I teased, kissing the side of her neck as I pushed her top knee forward. I loved waking up with easy access to her.

Heather usually slept on her side. Sometimes I'd wake up on my back with her pressed against my chest, and other times I'd wake up with her facing away from me and my dick nestled in the crack of her ass. I was pretty sure she slept however she was comfortable and I was the one moving to be closer to her.

"I was on a deserted island," she said with a sigh as I rubbed back and forth over her pussy from behind. "And I was rolling around on the sand with… Jason Momoa."

I scoffed and slapped gently at her pussy, making her jerk in surprise. "Wrong answer," I mumbled, making her laugh.

"I wasn't even—" her words cut off as I lined up my cock and slid inside her. It was still a tight fit, fantastically tight, but her body had grown used to me and it only took a couple thrusts before I was all the way inside.

The sex was lazy, all small movements and soft touches, but it was just as good that way as it was when we were rolling around all over the bed. I'd never had that with someone else. Get in, get off, get out had been the status quo since I'd started having sex. I'd never done the slow stuff until Heather. I'd never really wanted to, and I also had only woken up with women a handful of times.

"You should go," Heather murmured as I pulled away, making me frown. "We're not supposed to see each other before the wedding."

"I think that ship has sailed," I replied, grabbing a t-shirt off the floor to clean her up.

I really needed to stop being inside her without a condom, even if I was pulling out before I came. That worked most of the time, but it sure as hell didn't work all the time. She was on birth control, but I'd heard people say it sometimes didn't work for one reason or another, and I wasn't a fucking doctor so I had no idea what those reasons were.

"I'm getting ready at Brenna's," Heather said, rolling over to face me as I got out of bed. "As soon as I'm showered and stuff I'm going to go over there."

"You need me to do anything?" I asked as I walked over and started some coffee.

"No. Did you get clothes yesterday?" She sat up in bed and leaned back against the headboard, pulling the blankets up to her chest.

"Yup."

"We have to have two people sign as witnesses, I was thinking my sister and your brother?"

"Fine with me."

"I forgot to get you a ring," she blurted suddenly, her eyes going wide. "Shit."

"Wouldn't wear one anyway." I shrugged.

"What? Why?"

" 'Cause I'm workin' on cars all day. Wedding ring gets caught inside an engine with my finger still in it and I'm fucked."

"Oh. That makes sense."

I poured her a cup of coffee and carried it over, kissing her before I'd let her have it. "It's gonna be great," I said, kissing her again. "Stop worryin'."

Heather stayed in bed while I hopped in the shower, but she was already getting her stuff together when I came back out of the bathroom. I stopped for a second in the doorway and stared. Her hair was crazy; she had some little indented lines across her hip from where she'd been lying on the sheets, and she was bent over searching for something under the bed with her bare ass in full view.

"You need some help?" I asked, startling her.

"Shit," she muttered, straightening up quickly. "Did you get a good show?"

"It was pretty nice," I teased, dodging the balled up sock she threw at me.

"Do you have more stuff to bring over tonight?" She glanced at my duffle bag. "I was thinking I'd make some space before I left today."

"Nah." I shook my head, moving forward so I could get my hands on some of the naked skin she was flaunting. "That's pretty much all of it."

"You only have one bag full of stuff? Seriously?" she asked, resting her hands against my chest as I pulled her against me.

"Nova's stored at my parents. So's the shit from when I was a kid and all my campin' stuff. Tools are at the garage."

"Well that makes things easy," she said with a smile. "Now go. I need to get ready."

I leaned down and kissed her, sliding my tongue into her mouth as her fingers gripped my t-shirt. I'd just had her and I already wanted her again. It was fucking nuts.

"Go," she ordered, pushing me back a step.

I nodded and let go of her, but I didn't move as she slid around me and closed herself into the bathroom.

I was getting married.

Holy fuck.

She popped her head back out the door and gave me a small smile. "I'll see you soon."

"Yeah you will."

Chapter 11

HEATHER

"Stop moving!" Farrah griped as she tried to get my new diamond stud through my top lip.

"I'm trying," I mumbled back.

"Stop talking! Jesus!"

"Are you guys almost ready?" my sister asked, walking into Brenna's kitchen. "You're going to be late."

"We on a timeline?" Farrah asked dryly.

"Well, everyone is here."

I pulled my head away from Farrah as soon as she'd secured the jewelry and looked up at my sister.

"Whoa, sisterbeast," she said, smiling wide. "You look beautiful."

"Try not to sound so surprised," I joked, getting to my feet.

I'd tried on my dress when we were at Farrah's the night before, and thankfully it fit me like a glove. I couldn't wear a bra with it, but I was pretty sure Tommy would dig that, so I didn't worry about it. Farrah had curled my hair away from my face in soft waves and stuck the headband on so it just peeked out at the top of my head, but I hadn't let anyone help me with my makeup. I'd done it myself, knowing what worked and what didn't after my trial and error the night before. My eyes were done in nudes with thick black winged liner and a ton of mascara, and I'd covered my lips in a deep plum color that matched my fingernails. It ended up looking a little retro and a little rocker and completely rad.

"Who's here?" I asked Mel, picking up my train so it wouldn't drag across the floor.

"Mom and Dad." She rolled her eyes. "And Aunt Kathy, Uncle Randy and Devin."

"What?" I asked, freezing in place.

"What?" Mel asked in confusion as Farrah stood up from her seat and grabbed my elbow like she thought I was going to fall.

"Who the fuck invited them?" I asked, pulling away from Farrah so I could hurry to the front door. "We need to get over there right now."

Farrah and Mel were the only ones left in the house and I didn't pause to wait for them as I stormed outside and got in the passenger side of Farrah's car. The plan had been to walk through the field between the house and the club, but I was suddenly afraid that would take too long.

Thankfully Farrah must have understood my urgency because she was right behind me and got us over to the clubhouse fast.

I didn't bother walking through the building, instead I hurried around the side. I could hear a bunch of voices talking and laughing out back, and I let out a relieved breath as I went around the corner and found everyone calmly standing around. Kids were running around the chairs that had been set up, and there were a group of guys getting beer from a keg set up next to the building. I searched the crowd for Tommy and found him up near the front of the chairs, laughing at something Leo said to him. I grinned and started to take a step backward so no one would see me when Tommy's smile suddenly dropped off his face.

At first he looked confused, like he couldn't quite place the person he was looking at, but it only took a second before his face tightened in anger. I'd seen Tommy mad plenty of times, but I'd never him livid. It was practically rolling off him as he stepped forward.

I glanced to where he seemed to be looking and my stomach sank. My parents were standing in a little group with my aunt and uncle, and right in the middle of them was Devin. Even though Mel had told me he was there, I hadn't quite believed her until I saw him with my own eyes.

"Tommy," I said as he continued to move through the crowd. He didn't hear me so I said it a little louder, trying to get his attention, but it was no use. He was headed straight for Devin, and by the look on his face he was going to kill my cousin.

"Tommy!" I yelled again, catching the attention of Will and Casper who were just ahead of me.

I picked up my skirt and rushed forward just as the men turned to look at me. Something must have shown on my face because without a word they were turning to look for Tommy in the crowd and were suddenly jogging toward him.

"Tommy," I said again, trying so hard not to make a scene as I pushed through the crowd. People were starting to notice me, and everyone had grown quiet by the time Will grabbed his brother around the chest and yanked him backward.

I couldn't hear what Will was saying into Tommy's ear, but it didn't seem to be making a difference. My future husband pulled so hard against his brother's arms that the tendons in his neck were bulging. He didn't even seem to register the people around him that were rounding up the kids and ushering them back inside. He just stared straight at Devin, who consequently looked like he was going to piss his pants.

"Thomas," I said when I was finally close enough for him to hear me.

"Stay back," Will warned, his arms flexing as Tommy pulled against them.

I snorted and moved closer until I was right in front of them.

"Hey," I said, reaching up to put my hands on his cheeks. "Tommy."

He looked down at me in surprise and his body relaxed a little, but not much.

"How do I look?" I asked, giving him a small smile.

"Beautiful," he said softly, turning his head to kiss one of my palms before his eyes shot back up to my cousin.

"You need to calm down," I murmured, rubbing my thumb over his jaw. "I can't marry you if Will can't let you go."

"That motherfucker—"

"I know, baby," I said, moving even closer and making Will curse. "We'll make him leave."

"He shows his face at our goddamn wedding?" he growled, jerking at Will's arms. "Motherfucker didn't learn his lesson the first time."

"Tommy," I snapped, making his eyes meet mine again. "I'm not playing with you. Calm your ass down so we can get married or I'm leaving your ass at the altar."

"You think I'm gonna let that piece of shit walk away again?" he argued.

"I think you're going to stand here with me," I replied, ignoring the sound of disbelief he made. "And your brother is going to go tell him he's not welcome here."

"Not happenin'," Tommy spit out, jerking against his brother's arms.

"Alright," I said, dropping my hands from his face. "Then Will's going to hold you while I go tell him—"

"You take one step in his direction," Tommy warned, his eyes meeting mine again. "One fuckin' step, Heather—"

"Then you have to stop," I said quietly. "You need to calm down if you don't want me to go over there."

He glared at me, his nostrils flaring, but slowly his body started to relax.

"Thank you," I whispered, reaching out again.

Just as my hands made contact with his chest, he yanked away from Will who'd loosened his hold. For a second, my heart stopped, but then his arms were around me, pulling me up until my feet no longer touched the ground.

"Get him outta my sight," he growled at his brother.

After that, there was a commotion behind me but I didn't try to turn and watch. I could hear my uncle and aunt protesting as Will pushed Devin through the crowd, but I didn't care. They didn't matter. The only thing that mattered to me in that moment was calming the man whose arms around me were shaking with fury.

"I told you not to do that shit," he growled, his arms tightening. "I fuckin' told you."

"It worked, didn't it?" I asked smugly, letting out a yelp when he dropped me abruptly to my feet.

"You fuckin' kiddin' me right now?" He took a step back and suddenly, I was cold. Really cold. "It's the one thing I fuckin' asked!"

"Shut up, Thomas," I spat, crossing my arms. "The *only* thing you get to say to me right now is how pretty I look."

"You know you look gorgeous," he snapped back, running his fingers through his hair.

He was pissed, but I could see the tension slowly leaving his shoulders once my cousin was out of his sight. I swallowed hard, the shock of the entire situation finally hitting me. I'd seen people angry plenty of times. I'd even seen the Hawthorne temper on full display before. But I'd never seen anything like Tommy when he'd seen Devin. He'd looked possessed. And like it usually happened when I got myself into shit without thinking it through, once it was over I began to freak out.

I was just about to open my mouth to say God knows what, probably something stupid, when Molly came up beside me and wrapped her fingers around my arm.

"We ready to do this the right way?" she asked drolly, glancing between Tommy and me.

"Yeah," I rasped, nodding my head. I turned away and began to walk back toward the building when Tommy called out.

"Hey, sugar," he said, roughly. "I'll see you soon, yeah?"

My lips twitched and the nervous knot in my stomach unraveled as the words I'd said to him that morning came back to me.

"Hell yeah, you will," I replied, glancing back over my shoulder.

He gave me a small grin and nodded once.

Then it was time for everyone to sit down so I could make my grand entrance…again.

★ ★ ★

"YOU LOOK HOT as fuck in this dress," Tommy said a few hours later, his hands skimming down my back to grip my ass as we swayed from side to side.

They hadn't set up a dance floor, but there was music pouring out of a pretty incredible sound system and we were at the edge of the crowd enjoying the little bit of privacy we'd finally found.

"Thanks," I said with a chuckle. "But not exactly what I was going for."

"Stop," he mumbled, leaning down to kiss me softly. "You look beautiful."

I grinned.

"You just also look like you'd enjoy me bending you over and taking you hard."

The grin fell off my lips and I smacked his chest. "Jesus, Tommy!"

"What?" he asked, laughing. "It's all legal now."

"It wasn't illegal before," I muttered, twisting in his arms until my back was nestled against his front.

"Do you think this is going to work?" I asked as I watched his family and friends visiting and laughing in small groups all over the yard.

"Do you think it'll make any difference?"

"Will it keep me out of jail?" he asked. I nodded.

"Probably not," he said, gripping me tighter so I couldn't turn around to argue. "But if it comes to that, they can't make you testify and I'll know you're taken care of out here."

"I don't need protection," I murmured, lifting a hand to wrap around his forearm.

"It'll make me feel better that you are," he murmured back, kissing my temple. "Got a feelin' that somethin' with the Russians is brewin'."

"Why do you think that?" I asked, leaning back against him. He was wearing a black button down under his leather vest, and I could feel the buttons pressing against my bare back.

"Just tension around the clubhouse," he replied. "Somethin' ain't right."

"They'd say something, though, wouldn't they?"

I glanced around the crowd, picking out the faces I knew. My parents had left right after the ceremony, but Tommy's parents were still there, laughing at something Farrah was saying. Her husband Casper was shaking his head, but he was grinning, too. Will was dancing with Molly, Rebel pressed in between them, and Leo was twirling a giggling Lily around while Cecilia did the same to one of Trix's boys. They all seemed to be having a good time, and from the outside it didn't look like anything was wrong. But as I looked closer, I noticed that at any time there were at least a few men missing from the festivities. They'd show back up for a while, but others would leave. Almost as if they were taking shifts.

"Don't keep me in the loop," Tommy said in frustration. "But don't worry."

"I'm not worried," I lied quickly, my stomach knotting.

At some point, between the commune living and the wedding shopping, I'd come to care for the people out there in the yard. I'd wormed my way in somehow, and I couldn't see them as separate from me anymore.

"What did I tell you?" he whispered, nuzzling my neck. "Hmm?"

"You'll take care of me," I muttered in mock irritation, giggling a little as he tickled me.

"That's right," he promised. "I'll take care of everything."

With one last kiss against my neck, he pulled away and tugged me toward the rest of the party.

"I thought you'd dragged the poor girl off," Casper called out as we crossed the blackened grass.

"Nah, not yet," Tommy joked. "She's only gettin' one wedding, so I figured we'd stay a while."

I squeezed his hand in annoyance, but he ignored me.

"I think I need my septum done again," Farrah announced, staring at my nose.

"No you don't," Casper replied. "We're too old for that shit."

"Speak for yourself!"

"Baby, you're older than I am," he said, making her gasp in indignation.

"Guess who isn't gettin' laid tonight," Grease muttered into his beer, making a giggling Callie elbow him in the side. He raised his eyes to me. "Welcome to the family."

I snorted, but couldn't help but smile at the way Farrah was glaring at her husband. He seemed to be sober, but she definitely wasn't, and as she glared he just stared back at her calmly, a little grin tugging at the corner of his mouth.

"Wilfred!" she called, raising her arm to wave it at Will. "Who's older, your uncle or me?"

Will barely lifted his head from Molly as he called back, "Casper."

"Pussy," Casper mumbled, making Grease laugh.

"You want a drink?" Tommy asked me as he ran a hand down my

arm.

"No, thanks." I wasn't willing to risk spilling something on my dress. I'd stuff my face and have something to drink later after I'd changed.

"Thomas," Grease said before Tommy could walk away. "Here." He took something out of his pocked and handed it over.

"What's this?" Tommy asked, looking down at the little card in his palm.

"You shouldn't spend your wedding night at home," Callie joked, shrugging her shoulders. "You've got years to do that."

I looked down at the card and recognized the name written on it as a pretty ritzy hotel downtown. The room number was scrawled across the little paper sleeve.

"Thanks," Tommy said in surprise, glancing at me. "You didn't have to do that."

Grease cleared his throat and nodded. "Get started out on the right foot," he said gruffly.

The guy was impossible to read, so I didn't know if the gesture was a sign of approval… but it was still a really nice thing for him to do.

"Thank you," I murmured, meeting his eyes.

Everyone was silent for a moment. Tense. Then all of a sudden I was off my feet as Tommy slung me over his shoulder to the amusement of our guests.

"Tommy!" I screeched, making everyone laugh.

"This changes things," I heard him say as he strode across the yard. I assumed he meant the hotel key card.

"You gonna try to get her on your bike like that?" Leo asked in amusement as we passed him.

"Nah, I got the Nova."

"You're dead," I muttered as he rounded the building, never setting me back on my feet. "My boobs are falling out of this dress and I'm pretty sure I just flashed your dad."

"Lucky him."

"And Leo," I griped.

Just like that, I was back on my feet.

"That's not funny," he muttered, grabbing my hand to pull me along behind him.

"I wasn't trying to be funny. I'm not wearing a freaking bra."

"I noticed," he said with a small noise of approval.

It didn't take long to get to the Nova, and I cursed when I saw what someone had done to it. There were condoms taped all over it. They were everywhere, from the front bumper to the back window, and in every shade of the rainbow. Not the wrappers, either. The actual condoms. Hanging there like multi-colored deflated penis balloons.

"Assholes," Tommy chuckled, shaking his head. He went to open the passenger side door for me, but I took a step back and scoffed.

"I'm not riding in it like that," I said, glaring at the car. "No fucking way."

We started pulling them off, one by one, and the longer it took the more we started to laugh, until both of us were almost hysterical.

"My hands are covered in lube," I gasped out, tears streaming down my face. "This is so disgusting."

"Well at least they were concerned for your pleasure," Tommy retorted, swinging a ribbed condom from his fingertips.

"Oh my God, can you imagine if we took all these with us and then next week told them thank you, like we'd actually used them?"

Tommy roared with laughter, ripping a purple condom off the hood. "That's happenin'," he announced with a nod, trying to catch his breath. "Fuck, they better not have fucked up my paint."

Twenty minutes later we were flying down the highway with a pile of what looked like used condoms in a gooey mess on the back floorboard.

Chapter 12

THOMAS

"Y OU REALIZE WE won't be sleeping here, right?" I asked Heather, pausing in front of our hotel room door.

"What?" she asked distractedly, looking around the fancy hallway. I waited, watching as she took everything in, then tried to keep a straight face as her wide eyes met mine. "What?" she asked again, this time in disbelief.

"We're not sleeping here," I said again, letting that sink in as I opened the door for her.

"Why the hell not?" she protested as she pushed past me into the room.

I stepped in behind her and let the door swing shut as I reached out to grip her hips. "Because we won't be sleeping," I murmured in her ear.

I wrapped one arm around her waist and used the other to lift her legs off the floor, laughing at her surprised yell. The bed was massive and when I dropped her down in the middle of it, I couldn't help but smile at the picture she made. The hotel we were in was an old one. Old and fancy. And she looked like some movie star from the forties with her hair all curled up and her old-fashioned dress on, lying in the middle of that fancy ass four-poster bed.

"Wow," I said, looking her over.

She lifted her arms until her head was resting on her hands and bent her knee, making her dress slip all the way up her thigh.

"It's about time you noticed," she said smugly, relaxing back against the bed.

"Oh, I noticed," I mumbled, dropping my cut on the floor.

Usually I was more careful with the leather when I took it off, but I couldn't look away from her long enough to find somewhere to set it down. There was something about the fact she was my *wife* that made her infinitely more attractive. I hadn't even known it was possible to want her more than I already had. I thought about her constantly, no matter what I was doing, but when we'd been saying our vows, something had shifted.

I'd already claimed her at the club, but this was different. What had seemed like just a piece of paper before had somehow solidified into something way bigger and way more important than that. She was mine. She could leave me at any time, walk away and never look back, but the fact would remain that at some point I had been her husband. She'd stood up before a group of people, her parents and mine, and made that commitment to me.

And I'd made that commitment, too.

I knew without a doubt, no matter what happened or how things played out, I'd always keep that promise. She could always depend on me. Even if she left. Even if down the road we decided we couldn't do it anymore. If she needed something, I'd do my damnedest to make it happen. Always.

"You're staring," she said softly, pushing herself up on her elbows.

"You're my wife," I replied, just as quiet.

I unbuttoned my shirt as I watched her, taking in the rise and fall of her chest and the way she fluttered her feet to kick off the flip flops she'd worn under her dress.

"You're my husband," she replied with a huge grin.

I shrugged my shirt off my shoulders, and felt my chest puff out a bit at the way her eyes followed the movement, her head tilting to the side just a little, like she was trying to see me from every angle. Then as I was unbuckling my belt, her eyes dropped, and her tongue swept along her bottom lip... and I was done. What little reserve I'd had disappeared and within seconds my jeans and boxers were around my ankles while I tried like hell to get my boots off.

Heather giggled as I lost my balance and fell sideways onto the bed with a curse.

"Need some help?" she chirped, grabbing handfuls of her dress and hiking it up so she could crawl on top of me.

I rolled to my back and groaned as she lowered herself onto me, her pussy rubbing against my stomach.

"You got nothin' on under that?" I asked in surprise. I dropped my head to the bed as I gave up on my boots and reached for her instead.

"Nope," she answered, rolling her hips just once. "I figured if I wasn't wearing a bra, I might as well make it a matched set."

"You stood up there in front of the entire damn club and said wedding vows with nothin' on underneath your dress?" I slid my hands under her dress, and ran my fingers over her ass.

"Yep."

"I think I might love you," I said, staring up at her smiling face. I froze for a second, pissed that I'd blurted that shit out, but her grin didn't even flicker.

"Of course you do," she said, bouncing a little. "Everyone loves me."

We ended up fucking right there, with my pants around my ankles, boots pressed firmly against the floor and her wedding dress sliding over my skin as she rode me.

★ ★ ★

"WHAT ABOUT MEDICAL insurance?" I asked as I flipped on my blinker.

We'd woken up that morning—yeah, we'd eventually slept—and as soon as we'd checked out of the hotel we'd started going over shit that we probably should have figured out before we'd gotten married. Things like where we'd live, how we'd split expenses, if we wanted a joint bank account or not, and finally insurance.

"I'm on my parents' plan."

"Don't think you can do that once you're married," I pointed out, glancing at her. "I'll put you on mine. We've got full coverage."

She laughed.

"What?"

"You guys have full medical coverage?" she asked through her giggling.

"Yeah, dental, too."

She laughed even harder.

"It's a fuckin' business," I explained, shaking my head. "The garage has health benefits for the employees—would you knock it off?"

"Sorry," she gasped, trying to hold a straight face. "Sorry."

"You're gonna be happy for it, next time you get a cavity," I mumbled, making her snort.

"I've got awesome teeth," she informed me, opening her mouth as wide as she could. "See?"

"Yeah, yeah." I smiled at her and then scowled as red and blue lights started flashing behind me.

Son of a bitch.

"What the hell?" Heather said, turning in her seat as I pulled to the side of the road.

"Turn around," I ordered, grabbing my wallet and registration. "Don't say shit."

"What do you think I'm going to—"

"Not a fuckin' word, Heather," I warned as I rolled down my window.

She may have been pulled over before. Hell, knowing her, she may have even been picked up before. But she'd never been pulled over in a car that an Ace was driving.

"License and registration," the cop said, standing a little bit behind me at the window.

I handed it out with a nod, then set my hands back on the steering wheel as the cop walked back to his car. I didn't move. Any shift in my position could make the guy nervous, and I sure as shit didn't want to make him nervous with Heather sitting next to me. I watched him in the rearview mirror, and the minute he stepped back out of his car I fucking *knew*.

"Take the Nova straight to the clubhouse," I told Heather as the cop walked back toward us. "And don't say a motherfuckin' word to this cop."

"What?" she asked, her voice shaking.

"Sir, can you step out of the car?" the cop asked.

I took a deep breath and nodded, reaching out the window to open the door from the outside. Jesus Christ, they were picking me up the day after my wedding.

A few minutes later when I was face down on the hood, my hands being cuffed behind me, I was thanking God they'd picked me up the day after my wedding. I wasn't carrying for the first time in years. Even if they tore the Nova apart they wouldn't find anything. Everything was squeaky clean.

"Hey, man. Can my wife take the car home?" I asked quietly, staring at Heather through the windshield.

She was crying, one hand over her mouth as she watched the cop help me stand back up.

"Yeah," the cop answered. He was looking at her, too.

She was still in her wedding dress.

I winked at her as the cop walked me back to his patrol car, and after her initial shock I was surprised when she didn't jump through the window to throttle me. But that was good. I wanted her mad. She couldn't sit there on the side of the road crying her eyes out. I needed her to get back to the club and let them know I'd been picked up.

Apparently early that morning a warrant had been put out for my arrest for the murder of Mark Phillips.

I was banking on the fact that, without a body, their case was bullshit.

Chapter 13

HEATHER

"Let me the fuck inside," I ordered through my teeth as I rolled up to the gate. "I don't have time to pop the fucking trunk."

"You know the rules," the little jackass on the gate shot back, crossing his arms over his chest.

I looked around for some sort of lever but I had no idea if cars that old even had a trunk-popper thingie. I'd had a hard enough time driving with the fucking manual transmission. I knew how, but it had been years since I'd driven one. Oddly enough, I was pretty sure the last time I'd driven a stick I'd been in the Nova. Mick and I had stolen it and moved it down the street at a party so Tommy couldn't find it when he wanted to leave. We'd gotten to stay an extra hour that night.

"Fine," I bitched, climbing out of the Nova and stomping around to the back. I unlocked the trunk and threw it open, gesturing like a game show host and making the jackass roll his eyes.

"You're good," he announced with a nod, slamming the trunk closed again.

"I told you that," I growled, climbing back into the car. "Now open the fucking gate."

The Nova kicked up gravel as I made my way to the clubhouse, but I was too rattled to slow down. I'd heard the policeman reading Tommy his rights. Somehow they'd gotten enough evidence that they were able to arrest him for murdering Mark Phillips.

When Tommy had told me they'd never find the body, I'd believed him. He'd seemed sure. But I was terrified they'd found something else, some security footage or a fingerprint or a journal or something that would tie the two of them together. I had no idea what had even happened, so I couldn't speculate on what they might have found. Not knowing was terrifying.

"You okay?" the old guy Poet asked as I pulled to a stop and jumped out of the car. He was sitting on one of the picnic tables, but as soon as he saw the look on my face he pushed slowly to his feet. "Girl, you need help?"

"Grease?" I asked, looking around at the deserted parking lot. "Dragon? Grease? Casper?"

"Boys are inside, lass," he said gently, striding toward me. "Come on, now."

He placed his hand on my back and led me toward the open front door. As soon as we were inside he walked me toward the bar and tried to get me to sit down, but I couldn't do it. I couldn't wait.

"Give me a moment," he said firmly, nodding at me to stay put.

He rounded the bar and knocked on the door behind it before poking his head inside the room and saying something I couldn't hear. Then he swung the door open and took a step back as the men inside came out in a wave: Grease, Dragon, Hulk, Will, Casper, and a guy they called Samson.

"Heather? Where's Tom?" Will asked, stopping across the bar from me.

"He-he," I stuttered a little and swallowed hard. "They arrested him."

"Fuckin' hell," Poet muttered from somewhere behind me.

"They pulled us over," I babbled, finding Grease in the middle of the group and meeting his eyes. "I don't know why. We weren't going too fast or anything. And Tommy used his blinker. I know he did, because I always notice things like that and—"

"Breathe," Grease ordered softly.

I inhaled deeply and squeezed my hands together. "They pulled us over, and then the cop went to run Tommy's registration, and Tommy must have known something was up because before the cop got back he told me to take the car and come straight here and you'd know what to do."

I burst into tears as soon as I'd finished speaking.

"But what the fuck did they arrest him for?" Casper asked in confusion, raising his voice above my sobs.

"For murdering Mark Phillips," I rasped, raising my eyes to the men.

"Who the fuck is Mark Phillips?" Casper asked, clearly irritated he didn't know what the hell was going on.

"That teacher from the high school that went missing," Will muttered, scratching at his beard. "Why the fuck would they try to pin that on Tommy?"

All of their eyes eventually landed on me, and I froze like a bunny surrounded by a pack of wolves. "I have no idea," I blurted, digging my nails into my palms.

"We need a fuckin' lawyer," Dragon grumbled, reaching up to grab a bottle of whiskey off the shelf behind the bar. He twisted off the cap and took a deep pull before setting down a shot glass in front of me and filling it to the rim. "Drink it. You're shakin' like a leaf."

I picked up the shot and took it without protest, only spilling a little on my hand. Then I set it on the bar and slid it toward him. He filled it again and I nodded my thanks as I threw it back.

"How the fuck are we supposed to know anythin' if we don't have a goddamn lawyer?" Grease asked, leaning forward to rest his elbows on the bar.

"Well now, I can make a few calls," Poet said, patting his pockets as he walked away.

"He do it?" Hulk asked the group quietly.

"Where there's smoke," Casper mumbled, digging his fingers into his eye sockets. "Question is, can they prove it?"

★ ★ ★

Hours later, we were gathered around the bar once again. I'd curled up in Tommy's bed for as long as I could, inhaling the familiar scent of his sheets, but the minute I'd heard the guys congregating in the main room I'd left my safe haven.

"Talked to Nix," Poet announced. "Set me up with a friend. Attorney outta Portland. Says he's good."

"You know anything about this guy?" Casper asked.

"Just that my boy says he's good people," Poet replied.

"Wait," I blurted. "Who's Nix?"

"Poet's wife's kid," Will answered me as the guys continued with their conversation.

"Well, we'll feel him out when he gets here," Dragon said with a nod. "He headin' down?"

"When I called he said he'd be down Monday morning for the arraignment," Poet replied.

"Cuttin' it close," Grease muttered.

"Nothin' he can do before that," Poet pointed out.

The phone rang behind the bar and I startled. I hadn't even realized there was a phone there. Everyone was always using their cellphones.

"Yeah?" Hulk answered. He paused for a minute. "You wanna talk to your pop? Alright, she's right here."

His eyes met mine and my heart started to race. "Tommy," he called, wiggling the phone back and forth.

I slipped off my stool and raced around the bar, sliding in something on the floor and barely catching myself before I wiped out. I took the phone from Hulk and inhaled deeply.

"Hello?"

"Hey, sugar."

My eyes immediately started to water.

"Hey," I whispered back, turning so my back to the men. "Are you okay?"

"I'm fine. Done this shit before."

"Yeah, but—"

"They monitor these calls, baby."

"Oh." My mouth snapped shut.

"You okay?" he asked gently.

"Yeah. Yeah, I'm okay. I'm with your dad." I glanced over my shoulder to find Grease watching me.

"Good. Why don't you stay with my parents tonight?"

"What? No." I scoffed.

"Don't want you home alone."

"I lived there *alone* for months before your happy ass moved in."

"Heather, can you just sleep there tonight?" he asked. "Don't wanna worry about you, alright?"

It had only been hours since I'd seen him, but the exhaustion in his voice was clear. I immediately felt like shit for arguing with him about something that didn't even matter.

"Okay," I said quietly. "I'll stay with your parents tonight."

"Thanks, baby." He sighed. "I only got a minute. Can you put my dad on?"

"Sure." I turned around and motioned for Grease to come take the phone. "I'll talk to you soon, okay?" I said to Tommy. "Here's your dad."

As soon as I'd handed the phone to Grease I wanted to snatch it right back. Tommy was right there, on the other end of the line, and I hated that he was talking to someone else. I wanted to hear his voice again. I wanted to hear the sound of him breathing and the rustle of his clothes.

It was crazy how close we'd grown. I hadn't even realized how much I'd come to depend on him until he was suddenly out of reach. Somehow, in the midst of our secrets and deceptions he'd become my person. Like he'd said before, we were a team.

I walked to a couch across the room, ignoring the conversation happening at the bar. They weren't discussing anything I needed to know. Tommy was stuck in jail until Monday, but we'd found him a lawyer. I bent over and rested my forehead on my knees, letting out a shuddering breath.

There wasn't anything we could do until Monday.

"Come on," Grease called, walking toward me. "Thomas said you're stayin' with us tonight."

I lifted my head from my knees and then straightened completely as Grease got closer. "I can drive the Nova over there—" my words trailed off as Grease made a noise in the back of his throat.

"Even if my son hadn't told me not to let ya drive the Nova, hearin' the prospects laugh about how you were grindin' gears woulda convinced me to keep ya away from her," he said in amusement. "You can ride with me. Brought the truck in today since I thought I'd be haulin' shit to the dump."

"Are you sure it's okay with Callie?" I asked as I got to my feet.

Callie had always been nice to me and she'd practically invited me to live with them when I was a kid, but things were different now. She no longer had a house full of kids at any given moment, and I wasn't a teenager anymore, looking for a home cooked meal and a mother that paid attention.

"Yeah, it's all good," he replied gruffly, leading me outside. "I texted her when I got off the phone with Tommy. She knows you're comin'."

I nodded uncomfortably. As soon as we got outside I grabbed my purse out of the Nova and followed Grease to the little pickup he was driving. It was missing the front bumper and was two different colors like someone had slapped two trucks together and decided it was finished.

"It ain't pretty, but it runs," Grease announced as we climbed inside the truck.

The interior smelled a little like feet, and there were fast food wrappers all over the floorboard, giving me a pretty clear view of where Tommy had picked up his disgusting habits.

"You need to clean out your truck," I mumbled, pulling my seatbelt on. "This is disgusting."

"I want your opinion, I'll let ya know," he replied dryly.

"Seriously," I continued, like he hadn't even spoken. "This must be a hazard. One of these wadded up Taco Bell bags could roll to your floorboard and get wedged under the brake pedal or something."

"I'll take my chances," he said.

"I can't." I shook my head and searched around my seat, finally finding a crumpled up grocery bag between my seat and the door. "God, you gotta stop eating this shit," I mumbled. "Do you see this? It doesn't even mold!" I lifted up a breakfast sandwich and banged it against the dash.

"How the hell did I forget what a pain in the ass you were?" he asked, glancing at me.

"We tend to block out the bad shit," I replied, making a sound of disgust as I found an open ketchup packet on the floorboard. "Which is hopefully what I'm going to do the minute I step out of this truck."

"How the hell does my son put up with your shit?" he asked. "You bitch at him constantly?"

"No." I snorted. "He's easy to train."

Grease laughed. "All men are easy to train if their women know how to do it. Shit," he drew out the last word. "Callie's got me wrapped around her fuckin' finger. Wouldn't have it any other way."

"You guys have been together since you were kids, right?" I asked, picking up something unidentifiable off the floorboard.

"Yep." We flew around a corner and I swayed to the side, cursing. "Callie was younger than you. I was around Tommy's age."

"See, and you guys made it work," I pointed out. He was being nice to me, but I couldn't forget the asshole he'd been, and I had some sort of defect in my personality that made me unable to let shit go.

"Shit was different back then," he replied. "When Callie and me hooked up, it wasn't some big romance. Shit was goin' down and she needed me. Grew from there."

"Still," I mumbled. "You didn't have to be such a dick about it."

I hadn't ever learned the art of self-preservation either. Clearly.

"You come back to me after you have kids," he barked, not even glancing in my direction. "You raise 'em since they were babies, and when your son comes to tell you he's getting' married to a bitch he's been with for less than a week, you let me know how you react."

"Fair enough." I leaned back and looked over the now clean floorboard as I tied the top of the grocery bag. "But a little diplomacy would have been nice." I dropped the bag and looked at him. "And don't call me a bitch."

"I'll call you anything I want," he retorted stubbornly.

"No, you won't." I crossed my arms and stared out the windshield. We were almost to his house. "Your wife likes me and I'm married to your son. You don't want to piss me off."

"Big words for a little girl," he snapped.

"We're on the same fucking side!" I shouted, surprising him. "I don't really see why you'd be a dick to me at this point! Me and Tommy are married. The deed is done."

We were silent as we pulled up the driveway, but the minute Grease parked the car by their garage he spoke. "You've got balls," he said, nodding. "That's good. You're gonna need 'em."

"They're probably bigger than yours," I mumbled, reaching for my door handle.

"Hey," he called, making me look at him. "I ain't got no problem with you. Got problems with some of the decisions my son's been makin' these past few years, but I'm startin' to see you're not one of 'em."

"Good to know." I threw open my door and climbed out.

"Shit's gonna get harder before it gets better," he told me as we walked toward the house. "My boy ain't the same as he was."

"I barely knew him before," I replied snarkily. "I was always with Mick, remember?"

Grease scoffed. "Jesus Christ, girl," he said, shaking his head. "You don't know when to let shit go."

"Me and Mick were never a couple," I said as we walked onto the porch.

"Yeah," he murmured opening the front door. "I'm startin' to believe that. Pretty sure my sweet kid woulda turned into somethin' altogether different if he had to deal with your ass."

We walked inside and Grease called out to Callie that we were home while I looked around. The last time I'd been there, I'd been so nervous about telling them we were getting married that I hadn't taken in the changes they'd made in the past few years. Everything seemed less messy. There wasn't a pile of boys' shoes by the front door anymore. No backpacks at the bottom of the stairs. No spare car parts from the Nova or bags of chips and candy on the coffee table in the living room.

"Hey, sugar," Grease said as Callie came out of the kitchen. "Good day?"

"Until you told me my son was arrested," she muttered, leaning up to kiss him. "What the hell is going on?"

"I'll fill you in," he replied. "Nix is sendin' down a lawyer friend of his, so we'll know more Monday mornin'."

"I wish they were still young enough to spank," Callie said with a sound of frustration. "Damn it."

"I can do it for you," I cut in with a nod. "It's totally acceptable if I do it."

"Heather," she said with a smile, moving toward me. She gave me a tight hug and then leaned back, her hands still on my shoulders. "Honey, why didn't you change out of your wedding dress?"

I shrugged, looking down at my dress. It was wrinkled and sort of dingy looking from wearing it all day. "I didn't have any other clothes."

She made a sound of disgust. "You told me not to come down there," she bitched at Grease over her shoulder. "How everything was taken care of. You couldn't have gotten the girl something to change into?"

"Had some other shit on my mind, sugar," he replied as he pulled off his boots.

"Men are idiots," Callie told me quietly, shaking her head. "Come on, I'll get you something of Rosie's to wear. She's at Farrah's for the night."

She tugged me up the stairs and into Rose's room.

"We'll just get you some pajamas," she said as she walked to the dresser. "We'll go to your house and get you some clothes tomorrow."

"Thanks," I said quietly. "Uh, do you think Rose has a snug tank-top or something?"

Callie looked at me in confusion.

"I don't have a bra on," I said with an embarrassed laugh. "This dress keeps things in place, but I probably shouldn't be walking around your house with the girls loose."

Callie laughed as she rifled through Rose's drawers. "I'm sure we can find something."

As soon as she'd gathered up a pile of folded clothes, she ushered me toward the bathroom and waved me in.

"Take your time, our water heater is huge," she said with a small smile. "I'm making dinner, so just come downstairs when you're done."

"Okay." I smiled. "Thanks."

"You know," she said softly, "I always thought you'd marry one of my boys. I just didn't think it would be Thomas." She smiled at me again and closed the door behind her as she left.

As soon as I'd locked the door, I dropped down onto the closed toilet seat and stared at the wall across from me, trying to get my emotions under control. The bathroom was the same. It still had the same colored walls and the same raindrop shower curtain. There was still a little scent warmer thing plugged into the wall.

But it was different, too. Toothbrushes were missing. There weren't any wet towels hanging over the curtain rod. I reached over and slid the shower curtain open. There wasn't any boy body wash on the corners of the tub against the wall.

My eyes watered and I tilted my head back, inhaling deeply.

I was in a time warp. I'd taken showers, and brushed my teeth, and had once watched Mick putting on deodorant in that bathroom. I'd been in there a hundred times, yet it somehow felt foreign.

Everything was the same and everything was different, and I suddenly missed my best friend so badly it was a physical ache.

I stripped out of my dress and climbed into the shower, letting the hot water pour over my tight shoulders. I felt jittery. Like there was something I should be doing but wasn't. I knew I couldn't help Tommy. My job in that area was done the moment we'd signed our marriage license and I was no longer a threat to him. God, that sounded bad. There had never been any danger of me speaking against him. If my loyalty to Mick hadn't been enough to keep my mouth shut, my absolute support of Tommy taking care of Mark Phillips would have kept me quiet.

Tommy was so sure our marriage would work in his favor that I'd gone along with it, but I was scared it had only put a target on my back. The police could still question me, and I was sure they would. It was only a matter of time before they caught up with me and I knew I would have to answer the detective's voicemail at some point.

I finished showering and got dressed in Rose's pajamas, wrinkling my nose at the boy band faces on the front of the t-shirt. At least, I assumed it was a boy band. No guys were that pretty unless they were getting paid for it.

I left my dress hanging on the towel rack and went downstairs where I could hear voices drifting out of the kitchen.

"Is she okay?" I heard Molly ask, making me breathe in a sigh of relief. One of my people was there. I liked Tommy's parents, but their concern was Tommy. Molly, though, she belonged to me.

"She seems to be holding up," Callie answered. "She's doing better than I did the first time Asa got arrested."

"Wasn't the first time, sugar," Grease pointed out.

"Well it was the first time I had to deal with it," Callie said with a huff.

I rounded the corner and found Grease and Will sitting at the table, Rebel standing next to it, and Molly and Callie carrying dishes over from the counter.

"Yeah, yeah, you're such a badass," I said with a snort, making Will choke on whatever he'd been drinking.

"Keep pushin'," Grease grumbled, but his lips were twitching with suppressed humor.

"I would have been over earlier," Molly said as she came over to hug me. "But Will didn't think it was important to let me know what was going on until he got home tonight."

"It's okay," I replied as I gave her a squeeze. "There was nothing you could do anyway."

"Well I could have at least kept you company," she said as we sat down at the table. "You were at the clubhouse all day."

"I pretty much lied in Tommy's bed and stared at the ceiling the whole day," I said with a short laugh. "I wasn't good company."

"You did fine," Grease said. "Kept your head together, came straight to us, even gave your husband shit when he called. You did just fine."

"Were you listening in on our conversation?" I scowled.

"We all were," Will mumbled around a bite of homemade macaroni and cheese.

"Awesome." I shook my head.

"There's no secrets with that group," Callie laughed. "You think you're keeping things quiet, but everyone knows about them anyway."

My stomach lurched but I gave her what I hoped was an easy looking smile. "I'll keep that in mind."

"That's how they all knew you weren't pregnant," Molly said with a snicker, handing Rebel her macaroni sans cheese.

"We weren't even—" I snapped my mouth shut before I finished my sentence. Grease and Callie didn't need to know about my and Tommy's sex life.

"That's how they knew," Molly told me out the side of her mouth.

"You guys need to get a life," I announced, pointing around the table with my fork. "Seriously."

"Eventually, it gets better," Callie said from across the table. "They'll still know everything, but they just won't care as much."

"That's comforting," I mumbled.

"Asa, can you please pass the broccoli?" Molly asked, lifting her hand in a 'give me' gesture.

My mouth dropped open and I stared as Grease passed her the bowl of broccoli.

"Hey," I blurted, glancing between the two of them. "How come she gets to call you Asa?"

"Cause I *like* her," Grease mumbled, stuffing a bite of food into his mouth.

★ ★ ★

"Hey, you have everything you need?" Callie asked a couple hours later from the doorway of Mick and Tommy's old room.

I looked down and gave her a small smile from the top bunk of the old bed. I'd never been up there before. Mick always had the bottom bunk because Tommy had joked that if the bed broke, Mick would crush Tommy on the way down.

It was weird how things had changed. Years ago I wouldn't have gone near Tommy's bed, but when I'd gone in to sleep earlier that night, I hadn't even considered sleeping on Mick's bunk. I'd crawled up the broken ladder at the foot of the bed and immediately crawled beneath the covers.

"I'm good," I told Callie. "If I can fall asleep, I'll be perfect."

"I know how that goes," she replied, moving into the room. Then without a word, she disappeared from view and I felt the bunk bed sway a tiny bit as she settled into the bottom bunk. "I haven't been in here in a long time," she said quietly once she was settled. "I slept in here for a while after we lost Micky, but eventually Asa put his foot down and made me move back into our bed."

"Sounds like your husband," I mumbled, making her laugh.

"Well, he put up with a lot," she said ruefully. "I'm sure it wasn't easy taking care of someone with a huge surgical wound when she wouldn't get out of the bottom bunk of a bunk bed."

"Oh, shit," I said. "I didn't even think about that."

"It was…" she sighed. "It was the worst moment of my life. Asa and I had been through a lot by then, but nothing had prepared us for that."

"I'm sorry I didn't come to visit," I said.

"Oh, honey, don't be sorry." She paused. "I didn't expect to see you and I'm not sure I would have even realized you were there. By the time I was home from the hospital I was so out of it, I don't remember most of what happened afterward."

"Still," I murmured. "I should have stopped by."

"Well, you would have found a mess, I'll tell you that." She shifted on the bed, making the entire thing creak. "I was sleeping most of the time, Will was hovering like he couldn't figure out what to do with himself even though he was still healing, too, Tommy was angry and going off at the slightest thing, and Rose was silent unless she was up visiting Lily. I think Asa was the only one who was even functioning back then. I'm pretty sure he's never even dealt with everything that's happened."

"He's a do-er," I said.

"Exactly. When things are horrible, he's the one you'll see making sure life keeps moving. It's his way of processing things."

"Or not processing them."

"Or that," she agreed.

We were quiet for a while and just as I wondered if she'd fallen asleep, she spoke again.

"Did you know Asa got arrested when I was pregnant with Will?" she asked.

"I don't think I've heard that story," I replied, rolling onto my stomach so I could prop my head on my hands.

"We weren't living together then," she said with a small laugh. "I was stupid and I'd been putting off moving to Oregon from Sacramento."

"I don't blame you," I replied, making her snort.

"Anyway, he was headed down to see me and he got pulled over. He had some stuff on him he shouldn't have, and that was that."

"Damn."

"What made it even worse was that it was the day we did our ultrasound to see the baby. So there I was, waiting with my gram for him to show up at our appointment, and he never did."

"Oh, shit," I muttered. "Were you pissed?"

"Hell yes," she chuckled. "But I was worried, too. It wasn't like him to just not show up. Eventually Poet called and told me Asa had been arrested, but that didn't really calm my anxiety."

"I bet."

"He eventually got to call me and smooth things over a little, but it was a long time before I got over it. He ended up doing two years."

"Say what?" I blurted as I lifted my head in shock.

"Yep. I had Will while Asa was inside. It was a clusterfuck."

I choked a little at her words. "I didn't know that."

"It's not something we talk about a whole lot," she said easily. "I just thought it might help. You know, coming from someone who's been there. All of it may seem completely impossible now, but it's not."

"I think they're trying for a lot more than two years," I said quietly, closing my eyes as my throat tightened.

"They won't get it," she promised. "The boys'll do their best to make sure that doesn't happen."

I didn't reply. We both knew if things played out the way the district attorney wanted them to, there wasn't a damn thing the Aces could do about it. I was surviving on nothing but blind faith that Tommy knew what he was talking about when he'd said they didn't have any evidence.

We lay in silence for a long time, and just as I was finally dozing off a large shadow blocked the light pouring in from the hallway. I didn't lift my head as Grease moved toward us, but I did watch him through half-closed eyes.

"Come on, sugar," he said softly, leaning down into the bottom bunk. "You ain't sleepin' in here."

"I was keeping Heather company," Callie said as he lifted her from the bed.

"She don't care about your company when she's sleepin'," he answered, turning to carry her toward the door. "And I doubt she wants to hear your snorin'."

"I don't snore," Callie protested, tucking her face into Grease's neck.

"You sleep with me," he replied firmly. Then they were out of sight and all I could hear were Grease's heavy footsteps moving down the hallway.

I closed my eyes and told myself over and over again that Monday night I'd be crawling into bed with Tommy again.

Chapter 14

THOMAS

"I DIDN'T THINK I was gonna get bail," I muttered, glancing at my new attorney. He'd shown up in court that morning, surprising the fuck out of me with his slick suit and fancy fucking hair cut. I'd been dealing with a public defender for the past couple of days, and that guy had worn khakis and shirts that were two sizes too small and hadn't known or cared what the fuck he was doing.

"I'm good at my job," the lawyer muttered. "I'm parked over that way."

I followed him to his car and climbed in after him, rolling down the window so I could breath. I hated riding inside anything but the Nova. They didn't make cars that gave you room to breath anymore. Everything in the newer cars was crowded and full of levers and buttons. Fucking suffocating.

"Like I said inside, my name's Carter Lincoln," he said as he turned the car on.

"Nice."

"My parents liked the whole president thing."

"Obviously."

"My little sister is named McKinley."

"Mine's Rose," I replied, glancing at him. "Now where the fuck did you come from?"

"Owed a favor," he replied, pulling onto the highway. "Figured this was as good a way to pay it back as any."

"Not sure I can afford you," I muttered, looking over his suit.

"We'll work it out."

"Alright."

"I hear you just got married?"

I chuckled humorlessly. "Yeah, they picked me up the day after my wedding."

"You knew they were coming before that?"

"Yep."

"Smart," he said with a thoughtful nod. "You trust her?"

"Yeah."

"Good."

We were silent the rest of the way to the clubhouse, and I lifted my eyebrows in surprise as he made his way there without any direction from me. He'd obviously done his homework.

I waved my hand at the prospect on the gate and nodded my thanks as he let us in. I wasn't going to piss this guy off by asking to search his car. I knew he was legit from a conversation I'd had with my dad the night before, and I highly doubted he was trying to smuggle anything onto the compound.

He pulled to a stop and glanced at me to make sure he'd parked in the right spot, then shut off the car and climbed out like he fucking owned the place. No hesitation. He didn't even look around before leaning into the backseat and grabbing his briefcase. The guy was either a complete idiot, or had balls the size of watermelons. I was betting on the second one.

I turned my head as someone came out of the front door of the clubhouse and barely braced myself before Heather was jumping on me, her legs and arms wrapped around my torso.

"Oh my God," she whispered, stuffing her face into my neck. "You're back."

I met the lawyer's eyes over her shoulder. "My wife," I told him.

"I guessed that," he replied dryly.

I nodded and started toward the clubhouse, wrapping my arm under Heather's ass to support her. "Missed me, huh?" I teased, smiling when her arms tightened. "Told you I'd be out."

"Yeah, but for how long?" she asked darkly, not lifting her head.

"Not long if I woulda been stuck with that idiot I had before," I answered, leading the lawyer into the clubhouse. "But things are lookin' up."

"I'm pissed at you," she said.

"Why's that?"

"I have no idea, but I'm really angry."

I laughed and tried to turn it into a cough but I was pretty sure I hadn't fooled her.

"You gotta get down, baby," I murmured as I saw my dad, Dragon and Poet seated at a table in the middle of the room. "We got business to take care of."

Heather nodded, then pulled away from my neck, leaning back until we were nose to nose. "You haven't even kissed me," she said huskily, her eyes meeting mine.

"Didn't give me a chance to," I reminded her, reaching up to push her hair out of her face. "Come 'ere."

Her lips barely met mine when the urge to walk out of the room and find a little privacy hit me. I hadn't seen her in days and she'd been freaking out while I'd been gone and there'd been no way for me to help her. Her hands were shaking when she pressed them against the sides of my face and I couldn't help the groan that seemed to come up from my chest.

I stood there in the middle of the room, kissing the hell out of my wife until my dad finally barked my name in annoyance.

"Yeah," I answered after I'd torn my mouth away. "I'm comin'."

"Not yet," Heather whispered in my ear as she let her legs fall from around my waist. "But you sure as hell will be."

The lawyer I'd forgotten was there let out a little laugh and I watched her cheeks redden.

"You weren't supposed to hear that," she said. She glanced at him and then did a double take with wide eyes.

"I didn't hear anything," he said calmly, ignoring the way she was staring.

"Knock it off," I ordered as I gripped her hand and pulled her toward the guys waiting for us.

"I didn't do anything," she argued under her breath.

"Carter Lincoln," I said, introducing him to the table. "This is Dragon, Grease and Poet."

"Patrick," Poet said with a nod. "We spoke on the phone."

"Right," Lincoln said, reaching out to shake his hand.

I pulled a couple of chairs over to the table and motioned for Lincoln to sit, he sat down and I pulled Heather onto my lap, making him raise one eyebrow.

"Haven't seen her in days," I told him, ignoring the face he was making.

He nodded and opened his briefcase, pulling out the stack of notes he'd made earlier at the courthouse.

"You think you can get this thrown out?" my dad asked, leaning forward to set his elbows on the table.

"Easily," Lincoln answered. Then he smiled and I thought Heather was going to fall off my damn lap.

★ ★ ★

"You're not goin'" to any more meetings with the suit," I bitched later that night as Heather made dinner. "If you can't keep your damn tongue inside your mouth."

"Oh, whatever," she replied, throwing a carrot at me. "I wasn't that bad."

"Bullshit. I thought you were gonna pass out when he took his fuckin' jacket off."

"With good reason. Did you see that guy? He looks like a fucking model."

"Jesus," I muttered, pulling on a pair of boxers.

"Aw, someone's jealous," she sang, chuckling when she saw the scowl on my face.

"You wanna ogle somethin' I got somethin' for ya," I replied, reaching down to grab my junk.

"Later," she said with a laugh. "I'm still walking funny from earlier."

"Not my fault you jumped me the minute we walked in the door," I said as I came in behind her, wrapping my arms around her waist.

"Oh, please, like it wasn't a mutual jumping."

"Baby, your hand was down my pants before I'd closed the door," I teased, kissing her bare shoulder. "Pretty sure that was all you."

"I bent myself over the counter and pulled my own hair?"

"Nah, you were too busy moaning for me to give it to you harder," I joked, making her elbow me in the side.

"I'm just glad to be home," she murmured, leaning back against me. "I kept waking up thinking I was going to fall off your old bed."

"You slept on the bunk bed?" I asked, reaching around her to grab the plates she'd just filled up.

"Yeah." She grabbed a couple of sodas and followed me to the bed. "Your mom hung out for a while the first night, but after that I was on my own."

"They were cool about it, though, right?"

"I got into it with your dad," she said with a snort. "But I'm pretty sure I came out the victor."

"Sure ya did," I replied with a grin.

"Did you know Molly calls him Asa?"

"Yep."

"He doesn't let me call him Asa."

"I don't call him Asa either, if that helps," I mumbled, dodging when she threw a piece of food at me.

"Just so you know, if you go to prison I'm not moving in with them," she joked. I started to laugh, but when I looked up, her face had lost any trace of amusement. "You better not go to jail," she whispered through her teeth. "I'm going to be super pissed if you do."

"I'm not going to jail," I said, setting my plate down on the nightstand. "Lincoln's good. You should have seen this morning in court."

"I couldn't," she ground out. "He told us we couldn't come."

"He knows what he's doin'," I promised, pulling her between my legs. "If he didn't want you guys there, it's for a reason."

"I didn't think it would get this far," she said, setting her plate down so she could turn to face me. "I mean, I know we planned for it, but I didn't think it would actually happen."

"Ah, I knew you married me for my pretty face," I teased, resting my hands on her hips as she knelt in front of me.

"I married you because it made sense," she replied quietly, staring at my throat. "Because I wanted to protect you just in case."

"You're doin' that," I said, squeezing her hips. "You're doin' exactly what I need ya to."

"I need to call those cops back." She sighed. "And they're going to want to ask me questions."

"You don't know anything, baby," I reassured her. "Haven't told you anything for a reason."

"But I know enough," she said, running her fingers through her hair. "I know enough to make them go looking. Even if I say nothing, I'm afraid they're going to see something on my face or the way I move my hands or something."

"These are small town detectives, Heather," I replied. "This isn't *Law and Order*."

I sat there watching her freak herself out more and more, and had an idea.

"Get up," I ordered, pushing her back. "Get dressed."

"What?" She watched me in confusion as I pulled my jeans on.

"Come on, get up." I threw a shirt on and grabbed my phone, sending out a few text messages as she pulled some clothes on. "Grab a sweatshirt," I said. "We're taking the bike."

Twenty minutes later we were pulling back into the clubhouse. When I turned off the bike, she groaned and pinched my side.

"We just left this place," she grumbled as she climbed off behind me.

"Come on," I said, pulling her along.

I nodded to Poet who seemed to always be sitting at the bar, and smiled at Amy who was sitting next to him. Then I searched the room. My dad and Uncle Casper were sitting at a table talking, but looked up when I pulled Heather toward them.

"Hey, thanks for comin'," I said, pulling out a chair for Heather. "Sit, babe."

"Poker night?" Heather asked sarcastically. "I prefer Go-Fish, but I'm decent at poker."

"They're going to question you," I said, giving her shoulders a squeeze. "Both of 'em got lots of experience—" I glared at Casper when he laughed. "They can get ya ready, make ya less nervous."

"This is stupid," Heather mumbled.

"It's actually not a bad idea," my dad replied. "Now go away, Tommy."

"What?" I looked up in surprise.

"She won't be nervous if you're standin' over her like that. Waste of time to be askin' her questions if she's not shittin' her pants."

"You have such an awesome way with words," Heather said dryly. Then she tipped her head back to look at me. "Go. He's right."

"Alright." I searched her face, making sure she was okay with it, then walked to the bar and planted my ass on a bar stool next to Poet.

"Good idea," he said, nodding toward the group across the room.

"She was freakin' herself out," I replied, shaking my head. "Detectives already called her and she's been puttin' off callin' 'em back."

"They'll find a way to her eventually. Might as well get it over with before she pisses them off," Amy said, handing me a cup of coffee. "You want something stronger?"

"Coffee's good," I answered. "Thanks, Amy."

I looked over my shoulder and watched as Heather crossed her arms over her chest, then huffed and dropped them back to her sides. She sure as hell didn't look nervous yet.

"Poor timing for all of this," Poet said, twisting his glass of whiskey around and around. "Suppose it's never good timing, though, eh?"

"You know something I don't, old man?" I asked, knowing the answer before I'd even said it. Of course he knew more than I did. The man knew fucking everything. I watched his face carefully, but he didn't give anything away.

"All in good time," he said after a moment.

"Bullshit," I muttered, turning to look at Heather again.

Her shoulders were tight, and her hands were curled into fists in her lap as Casper leaned forward to say something I couldn't hear. Poet's hand came down on my shoulder just as I was about to rise.

"They ain't gonna hurt her," he reminded me. "You set it up, now let it play out."

I nodded, but kept my eyes on Heather. She shook her head once then huffed in frustration.

"The door was open," a voice called from the doorway, catching my attention.

"Come on in," I said, not bothering to stand up.

Lincoln walked across the room and smiled as his eyes met Amy's. "You must be Nix's mom," he said kindly. "He looks like you."

Poet snorted.

"No, he doesn't," Amy replied, reaching across the bar to shake Lincoln's hand. "But thank you anyway."

"Bone structure, mannerisms... your coloring's different but the way you carry yourself is pretty similar," he said as he held her hand.

"You seem to know my son pretty well," she murmured, glancing at Poet.

"You could say that," Lincoln replied. He turned to me. "Detectives want to question your wife?"

"Called her a couple days before the wedding and left a message. She hasn't called 'em back."

"Well, she should do that tomorrow morning," he said, sitting down on the barstool next to me. "The longer she puts it off, the worse it'll look, and you don't want them to change the invitation to an order."

"That's what I was thinking," I muttered.

"What are they doing?" he asked, watching as Heather threw her arms up in the air just as my dad leaned down and pointed in her face.

"The crucible," Poet said with a snicker.

"She was freakin' out about answering questions, so they're gettin' her ready," I replied.

"It's a good idea," he said and then looked at me. "But she doesn't need it."

"What?"

"I'll be going with her to answer their questions," he said simply. "As her attorney I'll be able to field most of their questions myself, and I don't need to practice."

Amy laughed evilly behind us. "I'm baking Nix a cake for this one."

"Do you want to go save her, or should I?" Lincoln asked in amusement as my dad and uncle played some fucked up version of good-cop-bad-cop and Heather flipped them off behind her back.

"I better," I replied, sliding off my stool. "If she sees you, she'll either start drooling or fuckin' pass out."

Lincoln laughed as I crossed the room.

★ ★ ★

EARLY THE NEXT morning I was up and dressed before Heather had even stirred. After taking time off the week before I needed to get into the garage and finish the cars I'd been working on. Customers didn't give a fuck if their mechanic got married; they just wanted their ride back when we said it'd be ready.

"I'm leavin'," I whispered, leaning down to kiss Heather's shoulder.

"It's too early," she groaned, reaching up to grab me like she was going to pull me back into bed. The offer was tempting as fuck.

"Lincoln's gonna meet you at the clubhouse at eleven," I reminded her, laughing as her arms fell back onto the bed dramatically. "You don't have to get outta bed for a few more hours."

"Thank God," she mumbled, rolling over and pulling the blankets over her head.

I smiled and grabbed my keys off the nightstand and headed out.

Her nerves seemed to have gotten better since the day before, but mine hadn't. I knew the detectives would question her differently than they had me. She wasn't suspected of anything, but I still hated the idea of it. They'd try to catch her in a lie. It was the nature of the beast, and she didn't deserve the way they'd go about it. I trusted Lincoln to take care of shit since he seemed to know what he was doing, but that didn't mean I wanted my wife getting questioned down at the police station.

"The hero returns," someone called out across the garage as I walked in twenty minutes later. Then everyone was clapping and cheering as I tried to keep a straight face. Fucking idiots.

My dad poked his head out the door leading into the clubhouse and lifted his chin in my direction. "Need a minute," he called out, disappearing again.

Shit. I took one more look at the car I wasn't even half done with and cursed. I was never going to get that fucker finished.

"What's up?" I asked as I stepped inside the clubhouse.

"Took a vote this mornin'," my dad said easily. "Patchin' you in tonight."

I froze. "What?"

"Congratulations," he murmured, grinning.

"Fuckin' finally," I muttered to myself, making him chuckle.

He wrapped me up in a tight hug and thumped my back a few times, then pulled away. "Get back to work," he said, still grinning. "You've been slackin'."

"Fuck off," I joked, shaking my head as I went back out to the garage.

"Congrats, baby bro," Will said, pulling me into a headlock the minute I'd stepped into my bay. "All grown up and becomin' a man."

"Fuck you," I bitched, punching him in the back as he gave me a noogie. "Get the fuck off'a me!"

He smacked me in the side of the head, then let me go, smiling huge as I shoved him away.

"Can I get some fuckin' work done, please?" I griped, grabbing my coveralls off the top of my toolbox. "I'd like to get done at a decent fuckin' hour tonight."

"Got big plans?" Leo joked.

"Yeah," I called back. "Gonna fuck my wife before I get my back piece and she can't dig her nails in for a while."

"Pussy," Will said.

"Shit," I replied. "Just don't wanna mess up the ink."

As the day progressed more guys came up to tell me congrats and make comments about the party happening that night. We didn't need a reason to party, we did that all the fucking time, but it was tradition to have one when a member was patched into the club. The old ladies were probably irritated as hell that they had to get everything ready, though. They'd just taken care of all the food and booze for our wedding and finally gotten the mess cleaned up.

At eleven I stripped out of my coveralls and met Lincoln out front as he pulled up.

"Ah, man," I joked, shaking his hand. "You're all slicked up again. Not sure how Heather's gonna be able to answer shit."

"Probably better that way," he said dryly, reaching up to smooth his tie. "Is she ready?"

I shook my head and looked toward the gate where Heather was just pulling in. "I'm trustin' ya, man," I said quietly as I watched her drive toward us. "Don't let 'em fuck with her."

"I'm good at my job," he replied.

I was at Heather's door as soon as she'd parked.

"Hey, husband."

"Hey, sugar."

She went up on her toes and gave me a kiss, running her fingers along my cheek. Then she pulled away and turned her head toward Lincoln.

"You ready, hotshot?" she asked, closing her car door.

"Whenever you are," he replied, his lips twitching.

She nodded and then looked at me again. "I'll see you in a little bit."

"Let Lincoln take care of things, alright?" I murmured, pulling her against my chest. "He knows what he's doin'. Let him do his job."

"Got it," she said, squeezing my waist before letting go. "Be back soon."

I watched her walk confidently to Lincoln's car and climb in with absolutely no hesitation and I realized... that's what she did. She could be stressing out for days about something, but the minute it was time for battle, she was completely composed. She made herself sick with worry, but when it came down to it she had nerves of steel.

I watched them drive away and crossed my fingers those steel nerves wouldn't desert her.

Chapter 15

HEATHER

"Let's do this," I announced as Lincoln parked outside the police station. "I'm ready."

"It won't be as bad as you're imagining," he said as we climbed out of the car. "I won't let them badger you."

"I don't even know why they want to question me," I told him as we walked toward the building. "Tommy and I just got together. I wouldn't have any information they'd want."

"We'll see," Lincoln said, holding the door open for me.

He escorted me to the counter and a man in his late forties came to greet us within minutes. "Hello Heather, I'm Detective Robertson. I left a message on your phone last week."

"Right," I murmured as I shook his hand. "You said you wanted to ask me some questions?"

"Right." He gave me a bland smile then glanced at Lincoln. "And you are?"

"Carter Lincoln," the lawyer said smoothly. "Mrs. Hawthorne's attorney."

The cops face retained the friendly smile but his eyes tightened. "I heard you just got married. Congratulations," he told me.

"Thanks," I smiled back, cool as a cucumber.

"Well, come on back," he said, leading us deeper into the police station.

I glanced around as we walked, but I didn't really see anything interesting. Men and women were mostly working on computers and only a couple of them glanced up as we skirted the room. The place was quiet. I'd expected something different, more exciting or intimidating or *something*.

"Come on in and take a seat," the detective said, gesturing at a doorway.

When I walked inside, it wasn't the room I'd been picturing in my head. Instead of a metal table bolted to the floor, there was a regular, wooden conference table. Some file cabinets were in one corner and a small coffee pot was sitting on the counter along the wall. It did have the mirror, though. It was definitely a two-way mirror. I wondered if there was anyone on the other side.

I sat down at the table and put my purse on the floor next to me while Lincoln got situated.

"I just wanted to ask you a few questions, Ms. Hawthorne," the detective told me as he sat down across from us. "You really didn't need a lawyer present."

"Mrs. Hawthorne has been advised by her legal counsel not to speak with police without her lawyer present," Lincoln said blandly, setting his folded hands on the table.

Detective Robertson cleared his throat in annoyance and gave a small nod.

"Do you know Mark Phillips?" he asked, without any build up whatsoever.

I looked at Lincoln the way he'd told me to the night before and caught his nod.

"Yes," I answered. "He was a teacher at my high school."

"And what did he teach?"

I waited for Lincoln's nod. "He taught English literature, I think."

"You think?"

"Well, it might have been creative writing. I don't remember."

"And were you in his class?" Robertson asked.

Lincoln nodded.

"No, I wasn't."

"But you saw him around school?"

Lincoln nodded.

"Yes. It isn't a very large school."

"And did you ever see him outside of school?" the detective asked.

Lincoln shook his head. "Mrs. Hawthorne's private life isn't up for discussion," he said flatly.

I swallowed hard as the detective's eyes narrowed.

The questions continued that way for over an hour. He asked me questions about my old high school, the schedules, the teachers, what year I'd graduated. I answered all of those. But any time he asked something that came too close to me personally, Lincoln shot him down.

It was like a tennis match. Detective Robertson would ask a question, and I'd look at Lincoln. He'd either nod or shake his head, I'd answer or Lincoln would answer, then we'd be on to the next question. Over and over and over. I had no idea how I would have managed it if Lincoln hadn't been there. Even after dealing with Grease and Casper the night before, I'd been completely unprepared.

When we finally left the police station, I was completely drained.

"You did well," Lincoln said as we walked to his car.

"Thanks. Holy shit, that was intense."

"Yeah, I had a feeling they'd go hard," he mumbled, unlocking his car.

I snorted at his word usage. He normally sounded so proper.

"I put in a motion to have the case dismissed," he said as soon as we were inside his car with the doors closed. "And I called the DA last night and told him the case was bullshit."

"Oh," I mumbled, buckling up. "You can do that?"

"Their evidence is nonexistent," he said in annoyance as we pulled out of the parking lot. "I'm not sure why they narrowed in on your husband, but they don't have anything on him. That entire arraignment was absurd. They had no grounds to arrest him."

"So they don't have anything?" I asked, turning to look at him. I'd barely heard a word about what was happening with Tommy's case. I knew he was trying not to worry me, but it pretty much had the opposite effect.

"Some kid saw Tommy and the teacher arguing in the parking lot of the school. Tommy slammed the teacher into a car, another teacher broke it up, and that was that," he said, glancing at me then back at the road. "But that can be explained away. Tommy's little brother and three other members of his family had just died. His mother and older brother were in the hospital. Not only is that enough of a reason for him to become…emotional, but if it went to trial, no juror would be unsympathetic."

"Yeah," I sighed. "That was a rough time."

"I'm sorry," Lincoln said. "I heard you were friends with the little brother. Michael?"

"Mick," I corrected. No one called him Michael.

"Right."

"Is that the only thing they had?" I asked as we turned up the road toward the club's gate.

"Everything else is circumstantial at best." He scoffed. "Tommy can't tell them where he was two years ago, because no one knows where they were two years ago. Mark Phillips had a stack of Michael Hawthorne's school papers on his home desk. Odd? Yes. But not outside the realm of possibility, the guy was a teacher."

My heart started to thump hard in my chest.

"They're scrambling. Trying to find something. They won't."

"Oh," I rasped, nodding as the prospect on the gate swung it open and let us through.

"The call will come in today," Lincoln told me easily. "They'll drop the case."

We came to a stop in the forecourt of the garage and I gave Lincoln a quick smile as I climbed out of his car. "Are you coming in?" I asked, grabbing my purse off the seat.

"No, I'm going to go back to my hotel and change."

I looked him over. "But why?" I asked. His suit was dark gray and it fit him perfectly from shoulders to ankles. He was seriously rocking the thing.

"Because this suit costs four thousand dollars and it's uncomfortable as fuck," he replied, loosening his tie.

I glanced over my shoulder when I heard Tommy call my name, then stuck my head back in the door. "It was worth every penny," I told the lawyer, smiling as he laughed. "Thanks, Lincoln."

"It's my job," he said with a nod.

I shut the door and turned toward my husband.

"How'd it go?" he asked, lifting me off my feet until I had to wrap my legs around his waist.

"Carter Lincoln's a badass," I replied as he carried me toward the building.

"Right? Dude is crazy good."

"He was all, 'Mrs. Hawthorne isn't answering any questions about her private life.' And the detective was totally swearing like a sailor inside his head, but he just nodded like he was resigned to it."

Tommy laughed.

"I would have been fucked without him," I said with a sigh as we moved through the main room of the clubhouse. "Casper and Grease were annoying and mean, but they didn't talk fast enough to prepare me."

"Oh, yeah?" he asked, maneuvering around the people crowding the room without once looking away from my face.

"Yeah. I'm just glad it's over," I replied as he carried me into his room and dropped onto the bed with me on his lap.

"Me too, baby," he said with a smile. "I got news."

"What news?"

"Patched in today," he told me with a smug grin.

"What? Are you serious?" I asked, looking down at the front of his vest. I ran my finger over the smooth leather where his prospect patch had been.

"Partyin' tonight, sugar," he said, grabbing my ass with both hands and bouncing me up and down.

I giggled as he threw me onto the bed and ripped off his cut, tossing it onto the top of his dresser. He turned back to me and wiggled his eyebrows before pulling his t-shirt over his head.

"Mr. Hawthorne," I said, wiggling my eyebrows back. "You're in an awfully good mood."

"Hell yeah, I am," he agreed, taking off his boots. "Got your shit taken care of, got that fuckin' prospect patch cut off, and now I'm gonna fuck my wife."

"There are people all over the club," I reminded him as he pulled off my sandals.

"Don't give a fuck," he replied, crawling onto the bed. He slid my dress up my thighs as he went until it was up around my waist. "And you don't give a fuck either."

"How do you figure?" I murmured, my lips twitching.

"Because you're not stoppin' me." He gave me a boyish smile and then his lips were on mine.

I ran my hands up his chest as he kissed me, feeling the scar on his collarbone from a fight with Mick when they were kids, and the long line of scar tissue along his ribs from a more serious fight he wouldn't tell me about. I'd come to memorize his body, the way he moved and the way his muscles flexed when he braced himself above me. I loved it. He wasn't bulging with muscles the way his brothers were, but each one was defined. Long and lean and mouthwatering.

He groaned against my mouth and pulled away, running his lips down my neck. As my hands roamed to his throat, he caught one hand and pulled it down between us. "Take 'em off," he ordered, snapping the side of my underwear.

As I reached down to push at the fabric, his hand went to his belt buckle.

"Fuck, you smell good," he said, sucking at my skin just above the neckline of my dress.

It took a little maneuvering, but it didn't take long before my panties were pushed to my knees and he was yanking them off my legs. His jeans were hanging open, and I reached forward and wrapped my fingers around him just as his hand slid between my thighs.

"Oh God," I moaned as he slid one, then two fingers inside me, curving them up and twisting a little.

"Condom," he murmured, nodding to the packet he'd set on the bed.

I closed my eyes and shook my head as his thumb pressed down on my clit. He was crazy if he thought I had the coordination to put a condom on him in that moment.

All of a sudden his hand disappeared and when my eyes opened in surprise he was watching me with a smile. "Fine, I'll do it," he teased, putting the condom on.

"I was busy," I said huskily, yelping in surprise as he suddenly grabbed my hips and flipped me onto my stomach.

I'd barely pushed myself to my knees when he steadied me with one hand and pressed inside me from behind.

I dropped to my elbows and inhaled sharply, clenching the blankets beneath me in my fists. Sex with Tommy got better every time. The more we learned about each other, the easier it was to push the right buttons, touch the right places and move in the right rhythm to drive each other crazy.

I stretched one arm back and gripped Tommy's thigh as he curled his body over mine, bracing himself on a fist near my head. He was surrounding me, his breath hot on my neck and his chest pressing against my back.

I let my hand fall off his thigh and reached between my legs, sliding my hand against the slick skin and using the heel of my palm to rub my clit as the tips of my fingers slid against his balls.

"Fuck," he groaned as he thrust harder, his fingers digging into my hip.

It only took a couple more thrusts before both of us came, first him and then me.

★ ★ ★

"WE REALLY GOTTA get up," he murmured, running his hand over my bare back.

He hadn't bothered taking my dress off until after we'd had sex, but the minute he'd pulled off the condom, he'd wanted my bare skin against his. I couldn't really blame him. I needed the closeness after the day I'd had, too.

"When is everyone showing up?" I asked sleepily, lifting my head off his chest.

"Most of 'em are probably out there already," he replied. "Boys'll come in when they're finished workin' and the old ladies'll come after that."

"And the side bitches," I mumbled.

Tommy barked out a laugh. "The what?"

"All the nasty girls that hang around." I said. "The side bitches."

"None of the men in my family have side bitches," he replied, trying and failing to keep a straight face.

"But the other guys do."

"Some of 'em, yeah," he said with a nod. "Doesn't have nothin' to do with us, though."

"That's bullshit."

"That's the way it is." He dropped his head back onto the pillow. "Don't go startin' shit, either."

"I don't start shit."

"Sugar, you're *always* in the middle of shit. Shit follows you around. Shit finds you and you wade in like Michael fuckin' Phelps."

"But I don't start it!" I pointed out.

"Alright, well don't get in the middle of it either."

"I'll try my best."

"Try harder than that," he said dryly.

He rolled off the bed and stretched while I stared. His skin was so gorgeous, perpetually tan and smooth. His whole family was like that. Lucky bastards. My skin was at least a few shades lighter than theirs, and it didn't matter what I did, nothing stopped me from breaking out in one spot or another.

"Get dressed," he ordered, putting an end to my ogling by throwing my dress at me.

I was silent as I put my clothes back on. Watching him move naked around the room unselfconsciously reminded me that there was a chance I wouldn't get to keep seeing him that way. Lincoln was sure the charges against Tommy would be dropped, and once that happened I didn't really see any reason for us to stay married. The police could always find a way to charge him later if they found more evidence against him, but I couldn't see that happening. They already had so little to go on, it was kind of amazing they'd singled out Tommy in the first place. I was pretty sure the district attorney wouldn't want to get his ass handed to him again by Lincoln.

"You ready?" Tommy asked as he stuffed his keys and wallet in his pockets.

"Yeah," I mumbled, running my fingers through my hair.

There wasn't any reason to start asking questions or try to figure out what we were doing then. It was the night of his party, the day he'd finally gotten what he'd been waiting for since he was a kid. I didn't want to ruin that.

When we got out to the main room, the place was already crowded and loud. Music was pouring out of the sound system, and smoke from people's cigarettes and pipes made the room kind of hazy.

"Looks different, huh?" Tommy asked, throwing his arm around my shoulder.

"Just a little," I replied, searching through the crowd to find faces I recognized.

"Come on," he ordered, leading me through the room. "Let's get a drink."

There were a couple women standing behind the bar I didn't recognize. They sure as hell knew Tommy, though.

"Hey, Tommy," they both said, almost simultaneously.

I rolled my eyes.

"Hey, can I get a couple beers?" he asked with a smile.

I pinched his side, hard, and I didn't let go until he gripped my wrist and pulled my hand away.

"Would you knock it off?" he said softly into my ear.

"Stop smiling at them," I ordered, making him laugh.

"Moose said not to give you beer," the bartender with long black hair chirped, setting a bottle down on the bar top. "Whiskey only."

Tommy laughed and grabbed the bottle. "Alright," he said. "My wife wants a beer, though."

Chirpy's smile melted off and she glanced at me quickly before nodding.

"You totally banged her," I accused, pulling out from under Tommy's arm. "Ew!"

"Does it matter?" he asked in confusion, twisting off the cap of his whiskey. "Wasn't plannin' on fuckin' her tonight."

My mouth dropped open in shock just as the chick we were talking about set my beer down on the bar.

"Thank you," I said politely, grabbing my beer. It really wasn't her fault Tommy was an asshole.

I turned back to Tommy and shoved at his stomach just as he was taking a drink, making him cough and choke. "You know, you're kind of sucking at this whole marriage thing right now," I informed him. "Get your shit together, Hawthorne."

I stomped away, but I wasn't really sure where to go so I ended up walking out front where there were more groups of people congregating. Everyone was joking and laughing like they'd done at our wedding, but the entire club had a totally different feel. Tommy's party was a celebration, but it had a darker edge.

Everyone was getting a little more drunk, wearing a little less clothing, and were talking a little louder. There was a fire burning in a big barrel in the forecourt, and there were at least fifty motorcycles lined up along the front edge of the building. Wives and girlfriends hadn't brought their family cars with the booster seats and airbags; they'd ridden in on the backs of their men's bikes.

I watched a woman climb onto one of the picnic tables and start shaking her ass and snorted. Then I realized it was Farrah.

I laughed as I walked closer to the table and tipped my head back to look at her.

"You're gonna break a hip," I called up to her, laughing and dodging as she tried to kick me.

"Little brat," she huffed, kicking at me again.

"Why the hell are you dancing on a table?"

"Because it pisses my husband off," she replied easily, giving Casper a little wave as he came walking outside.

"Like to do that a lot, huh?" I joked, watching as Casper stomped toward us.

"Aw, he loves me," she told me quietly, swaying her hips from side to side. "But he's been busy as hell, and if I don't piss him off he won't let loose tonight." She looked down at me. "Boys that don't let off steam once in a while end up dead from a heart attack."

"Is that your medical opinion?" I asked as Casper reached us.

His hand shot out and grabbed Farrah's wrist, and before I could blink he'd yanked her off the table and over his shoulder. He didn't say a word. Then they were moving across the pavement and disappearing inside the clubhouse.

I looked around but didn't see anyone I knew. Some of the guys were wearing vests, but they weren't Aces. I couldn't see the patches clearly enough to read them, but they were the wrong colors and shaped differently than Tommy's.

"Hello, beautiful," a guy said, swaggering toward me. At some point he'd probably been hot, but hard living had given his face a slightly sunken look that reminded me of a skeleton.

"Not interested," I said in amusement as he stopped and shifted his weight like he was posing for me.

"You seem interested," he said, looking me over.

I scoffed. "I'm not, Night of the Living Dead. Go away."

"You hear this chick?" Skeletor asked no one in particular. "You need to learn some manners."

"My manners are just fine," I replied, taking a step back as he took a step forward. "I told you I'm not interested. You just can't seem to take a hint."

"See, you keep talking shit, but your body, mmm…" He shook his head from side to side. "Your body is telling me you want it."

"Are you out of your fucking mind?" I asked dubiously, taking another step backward. I realized way too late that I didn't know anyone in the dark forecourt. There wasn't a single face I recognized, and most of the people out there weren't even paying attention to us. "That's the most idiotic thing anyone has ever said to me. *Ever.* And I know a lot of stupid people."

He made this weird noise, almost like a growl, and then he was hurdling toward me. I let out a startled scream and scrambled backward, but my sandal got caught where the grass met the pavement and I wobbled for a second before I fell hard on my ass.

He caught up to me before I could get back on my feet. His hand came down hard on my shoulder, but before anything else could happen something moved in the corner of my sight and the guy was tackled to the ground with a loud thump.

I crab walked backward as the two rolled around on the ground, then let out a little shriek as I realized what was happening.

Tommy.

At our wedding, I'd thought I'd seen Tommy in a rage when he'd seen my cousin, but it was nothing compared to what I saw when he kneeled above Skeletor and punched him hard in the jaw. The man I was looking at wasn't anything like the Tommy I knew. His eyes were blank as he wrapped one hand around the guy's throat and used the other to punch him over and over again.

Skeletor bucked and swung back, but the blows didn't even seem to faze my husband.

The sounds were terrifying. Thuds and smacks and the wet sound of blood and spit hitting the pavement and their clothes.

I pushed myself up to my knees, but my legs couldn't even hold me. All I could do was stare in horror as the guy on the ground grabbed hold of Tommy's vest and yanked him forward, his mouth gaping as he tried to bite him.

"Thomas!" Grease called as he and a few of the other men came flying out of the clubhouse.

They were on Tommy within seconds, but my husband didn't stop. He fought against the hold Grease had on him, yanking and twisting as he reached toward Skeletor again and again, finally kicking him hard in the ribs as the men pulled him away.

"Jesus Christ," Hulk said as he finally noticed me at the ground by his feet. "You alright?"

"What the fuck?" I whispered, my voice shaking. I gripped his hand when he reached for me, but the minute I got to my feet, my knees buckled.

What the fuck had I just seen?

Grease and Will were dragging Tommy back toward the clubhouse, but he wasn't going easily. He was rabid as he stared at the man being helped off the ground, but even scarier than that was the silent way he was losing his mind. He hadn't made a sound the entire time he'd beat the hell out of that guy.

"Come on, Hawk," Hulk said gently, lifting me into his arms. "Let's get you inside, yeah?"

I nodded as I watched Dragon walk up to one of the guys on a picnic bench, shaking his head.

Skeletor was on his feet again and was wiping at his face angrily as someone tried to help him. He shoved them away and turned toward the guy Dragon was talking to, throwing his hands up in the air.

Hulk carried me into the clubhouse, and I didn't even try to protest. My entire body was shaking and I could barely hear beyond the sound of my heartbeat in my ears. I'd seen men fight. I'd been to a lot of parties, and when people got drunk enough, there was usually someone that wanted to prove his dominance the old fashioned way. But I'd never seen anything as brutal as what I'd just witnessed.

That wasn't a brawl. If Grease hadn't come out when he had, there was a good chance Tommy would have killed that guy. Even the group of strangers had seemed hesitant to step in.

"Is she okay?" my sister asked, as Hulk carried me past the bar. She got to her feet and rushed toward us. "Heather?"

I couldn't answer her. My throat felt so tight I wasn't even sure I could speak.

"She's fine," Hulk said, stopping as my sister stepped in front of us. "We'll be back in a minute."

"What?" Mel asked incredulously, as Hulk moved around her.

"Rock," Hulk called out for my sister's boyfriend to come get her.

Then we were moving through the room and into the back hallway. As soon as we were away from the music I could hear Tommy.

"You stay right here," Hulk ordered, setting me on my feet. He opened up the door to Tommy's room and stepped inside.

"Where is she?" Tommy roared, making me flinch.

I slowly walked around the edge of the doorway, and when I came into view, Grease cursed.

Tommy stormed toward me and was knocked back against the wall when Will punched him in the cheek.

"Motherfucker," Tommy ground out, his eyes shooting to his brother.

"Stay the fuck there," Will ordered. "Jesus."

I reached out and braced my hand against the wall as I took in the room. Tommy's dresser was on its side, the wood splintered. The bed seemed untouched, but it looked like someone had used the tall lamp next to his bed like a baseball bat and there was glass all over the floor.

"Are you okay, sugar?" Tommy asked, his eyes on me. "You hurt?"

My eyes watered as I watched him try to calm himself down. There was blood everywhere. I didn't know if it was his or Skeletor's. His face was swollen and his knuckles were so torn up I could see the bone.

I shook my head. No, I wasn't hurt.

"The fuck was that?" Grease asked tiredly, dropping to the edge of the bed.

"Up!" Tommy ordered, moving forward until Will stepped in front of him. "Get the fuck off our bed."

I swallowed hard as Grease stood back up, looking at Tommy like he was insane.

"You wanna tell me why the fuck you just beat the hell out of the Rabid Dogs president's son?" Grease said lowly, his jaw clenched tight.

"That fuckin' tweaker?" Tommy asked, his eyes shifting back and forth from me to Grease.

"You think we invited them here for shits and giggles?" Grease asked, nodding at Hulk.

I stepped inside the room as Hulk reached behind me and closed the bedroom door.

"You think we want those fuckin' tweakers here?" Grease ground out. "We got shit in the works that you just fucked up. We need those motherfuckers to cut off the Russian's meth supply and now your president is out there tryin' to smooth shit over."

"He put his hands on my wife," Tommy spit, his nostrils flaring.

"Why the fuck was your wife outside *alone*?" Hulk said softly, making me stiffen.

"I wasn't," I said, my voice shaking. "When I went out there, Farrah was there. Casper came and took her inside. I—" I swallowed, trying to dislodge the lump in my throat. "She was out there by herself so I didn't know that I shouldn't be. No one told me."

"Farrah's well known," Will said, shaking his head. "No one wants to fuck with Casper so they steer clear."

The door opened behind me and I jumped, stepping quickly to the side as Dragon walked in and slammed the door shut again behind him.

"Someone wanna tell me what the fuck is goin' on?" he asked. The fury in his quiet words was chilling.

"Fucker put his hands on my wife," Tommy answered, his jaw tight.

Dragon looked me over then turned back to Tommy. "Looks fine to me. You wanna tell me why I just had to go kiss Sickle's ass so he wouldn't take off and ruin every fuckin' hour of work we've put in to get them on board?"

"I found her on the fuckin' ground with that tweaker on top of her," Tommy hissed. "The fuck did you expect me to do?"

"You alright?" Dragon asked, his eyes on me.

"I'm okay," I replied, crossing my arms to hide my shaking hands. "Skeletor just wasn't taking no for an answer. I tripped and..." I shook my head, closing my eyes as I remembered the way Tommy had tackled him.

"The fuck am I supposed to do with you, Tommy?" Dragon asked, running his hands through his hair and tightening the ponytail at the base of his neck. "Kept you a prospect until I thought you had your shit together, then you go provin' me wrong the same goddamn day."

"You woulda done the same goddamn thing!" Tommy spat back, his eyes bulging.

"Difference is, I can fuckin' get it under control before I goddamn kill someone in front of an entire group of people!" Dragon yelled back, making me jerk in fear.

Dragon quietly angry was scary, but when he finally raised his voice he was terrifying. I understood then why he was president.

"I just paid your bail—thank fuck you even *got* bail—for a fuckin' murder charge, Tom," Dragon said, his voice once again at a normal level. "You killed a motherfuckin' teacher. For what? You fuckin' lost it? You couldn't manage your temper enough to not kill a fuckin' polo wearin' poindexter? What'd he do, Tommy? Cut you off in motherfuckin' traffic?"

Tommy's head jerked back and his eyes narrowed, but he didn't say a word. He just lifted his chin in defiance and took it.

"Explain it to me," Dragon ordered ominously. " 'Cause at this point, it's lookin' like you need to be put down."

I whimpered as my eyes shot to Grease, but Tommy's dad didn't say a word. He just stood there staring at his son, waiting for his reply. The room was silent as I took in the men. Will was watching Tommy, his eyes practically begging his little brother to say something, and Hulk was expressionless.

"It wasn't like that," I finally whispered, my eyes filling with tears.

"Not another word, Heather," Tommy said through stiff lips.

"It wasn't," I whispered again, meeting Tommy's eyes.

"Don't say another fuckin' word," he ordered, his voice growing louder.

"He was bad," I said, my voice strangled.

"Heather!" Tommy roared. He took a step forward and Will shoved him back against the wall.

"Mark Phillips was bad," I choked out as Tommy completely lost it, shoving at his brother as he tried to get to me.

I shrank back against the wall as my eyesight grew blurry, but I didn't take my eyes off of Tommy.

"He hurt you?" Dragon asked quietly, ignoring the way Tommy fought with Will across the room.

I shook my head.

"Don't you say another fuckin' word, Heather!" Tommy screamed, his eyes wild.

"It wasn't me," I said, watching my entire relationship with my husband implode.

Hulk made a noise of disbelief, and my gaze shot to him as he shook his head and ran his hands down his face. "Mick," he mumbled. "Fuck me."

"What?" Grease asked, his face full of confusion. "What the fuck are you sayin'?"

Tommy roared and suddenly Will was flat on his back, one hand on his throat as he gasped for air. The room broke into chaos then.

I dropped to my knees and covered my head with my arms as Tommy threw punches, slowly making his way toward me as he fought every man in the room. I screamed as arms wrapped around me, but calmed as I heard Grease's voice in my ear. He carried me swiftly out of the room and the minute we reached the hallway we were surrounded by silent women, watching us in horror.

"You stay back," Grease ordered them, his voice shaking. "Let the boys handle it."

He moved toward the end of the hall and pushed his way inside another door, then froze in the middle of the room. He took a shaky breath, then another.

"Asa?" Callie's trembling voice called as she came in behind us.

"Come in, sugar," he ordered. "Close the door."

Callie followed his directions and walked around us slowly until she was standing right in front of us. I was still curled up in a ball with my arms covering my head, and even as Grease's breathing evened out, he didn't set me down. He just stood there with me in his arms, completely still.

"You're scaring me," Callie said softly.

Grease's chest heaved in what might have been a sob and he cleared his throat. "Sit down, Calliope."

He moved slowly and sat down on the bed, but his hold on me didn't loosen. He just continued to hold me tight as he rested me on his thighs.

"Heather," Callie said gently, running her hand down the back of my head. "You okay, baby?"

I shuddered, but didn't answer her.

How could I even answer that? I'd just watched the man I'd married completely lose control. He'd been coming for me and if the men in the room hadn't stopped him, I had no idea what would have happened. I didn't know that man. The Tommy I knew had never even raised his voice at me.

"You need to start talkin'," Grease said roughly, resting his chin on the top of my head. "But you just take a minute, girl. It's alright now. You just take a minute."

I let out a small sob, and bit my lips to stop any more sound from escaping.

"What the hell is going on?" Farrah snapped as she pushed inside the room.

"Get outta here, Farrah," Grease ordered.

"Hawk?" she asked, completely ignoring him. "Are you okay, sweetheart?"

"She's fine," Grease replied. "Shaken up."

"Casper's in with the boys talking to Tommy," Farrah said, closing the door behind her. "They're calming him down."

I whimpered and Grease's arms tightened.

"My son is not the priority here," Grease said softly.

I sucked in a desperate breath as I tried to get myself to stop shaking. I just wanted to be home in my apartment, away from all of those people. I didn't want to lift my head and deal with their concern. I didn't want to answer their questions or assure them I was fine. I just wanted to be alone.

I shifted and Grease's arms dropped as I straightened my legs. My arms were the last thing to unfold, and it was almost painful as I moved them away from my head. My biceps had muffled all sound, and when I dropped my arms down at my sides I could hear the music and people out in the main room of the clubhouse, partying like nothing was wrong.

I stood up on shaking legs, and put out a hand to stop Grease when he reached out to steady me.

"I'm okay," I mumbled, my eyes darting around the room. "Nice digs."

"Farrah," Grease said, ignoring my compliment. "Out. Now."

She looked me over and huffed in annoyance, then left the room, shutting the door behind her.

"Start talkin'," Grease ordered.

"Asa," Callie snapped.

"I ain't bein' mean," Grease said, watching me. "And I ain't angry. But you will tell me what I wanna know."

"Tommy," I murmured, glancing at the door.

"I ain't gonna let him hurt you," Grease promised, making Callie lift her hand to her mouth in horror. "But somethin's goin' on with my boy, and if you don't tell me what that is, there ain't no way I can help him."

I shook my head and stared at the floor, my mind racing. I'd kept the secret for so long I wasn't even sure I'd be able to say it out loud. I'd come close in the room with Tommy, but I didn't know how I could look at Callie and Grease and tell them what I knew.

"You said Mark Phillips was a bad man," Grease said roughly, his hand finding Callie's thigh. She laid her hand on top of his in support.

"Yes," I replied hoarsely.

"He hurt you?" Grease asked.

"No," I whispered.

"He hurt my son?" he ground out, his voice shaking.

I closed my eyes and sucked in a sharp breath, clenching my hands into fists. "Yes," I answered through gritted teeth.

Callie moaned.

"Which son?" Grease rasped.

I couldn't look at him. I could hear their unsteady breathing, loud in the room, and I couldn't even look at their faces.

"Micky," I cried quietly, the word breaking right down the middle.

I dropped my head in my hands and shuddered as I heard Callie start to cry.

"Michael was two hundred pounds of muscle," Grease said in a ragged voice.

I finally turned to look at him, and the devastation on his face nearly killed me.

This was why Tommy hadn't wanted them to know. Why he'd gone to such lengths to keep them in the dark. Why he'd been willing to go down for murder without saying a word.

"Micky was gay," I said quietly, dropping awkwardly to my ass in the middle of the floor. "He wasn't ready to say anything, but…"

"But he told you," Callie said softly, tears running down her face.

"He told me everything," I replied, nodding. "But I didn't know about Mr. Phillips."

"When did you know?" Grease asked, pulling Callie closer to his side.

"I found out at the end of the school year," I told him, staring at the floor beyond my crossed legs. "I caught them." I shook my head. "They weren't doing anything. Not really. But I knew just from the way they were standing that something wasn't right."

"That motherfucker," Grease said so quietly I almost didn't hear him.

"I made Mick tell me everything that night," I continued. "He tried to put me off, but I think he was afraid I was going to tell someone." My voice cracked.

"He was gay," I announced firmly, nodding my head. "That's what he told me first. He wasn't shy about it. It was like he was glad to get it off his chest. And it made so much sense, you know? I kind of started putting things together in my head and was realizing all the signs I'd ignored, but then he mentioned Mr. Phillips, and his entire voice changed."

The room was quiet as I tried to get my thoughts together. I almost didn't know how to explain the change that had come over Mick that night.

"He was *ashamed*," I finally whispered, shaking my head. "Whatever was going on with Mr. Phillips *embarrassed* him. He didn't want to talk about it, and he tried to say it was nothing, but I knew. *I knew.*"

"He was fourteen years old," Callie cried, shaking her head.

"It started midway through the year," I said, focusing on a knob on the dresser across the room. If I wanted to finish telling them, I wouldn't be able to look at them again. "And at first, Mick was kind of flattered, you know? This hot teacher was paying attention to him, and he liked it. But then it escalated, and Mick didn't like it anymore but he didn't know how to stop it. He just…" my voice trailed off. "He got railroaded into something by someone he should have been able to trust."

"Did he rape my boy?" Grease hissed.

"I don't know," I whispered, still staring at the dresser knob. "But he did *something* and it went on for months."

Callie cried quietly, but Grease was eerily silent. After a long moment, I lifted my head and met his eyes.

"I should have said something," I said, my voice thick with apology. "But he begged me not to, and I tried to protect him the best I could, and then… and then he was gone."

"You were a good friend to my boy," Grease said, his eyes wet. "He put you in a tough position."

"I should have said something," I whispered again. "I was older. I should have done something."

"Neither of you kids was prepared to deal with somethin' like that," Grease replied quietly, shaking his head. "We drill that shit into our girls' heads, but—"

"But we thought our boys were safe," Callie cut in. "They're so big and strong. By the time they hit high school, I didn't even…" She looked down at her hands. "I watched them closely when they were little, but once they were bigger than most men, I didn't watch as closely," she whispered.

I knew exactly how she felt. Mick had always seemed so strong to me. Even as a freshman, he'd seemed bigger than the rest of the guys I knew. He carried himself differently, was more aware of his body and the power it held. But looking back, I couldn't help but realize he was still just a kid. A really big kid. And he'd had no idea how to fight against the manipulation of someone older and well-versed in getting exactly what he wanted. I shuddered as I remembered Mark Phillips' face when I'd walked in on him and Mick. The guy hadn't even been nervous I'd found them together. He'd seemed almost smug. Like he was sure he would get away with it.

When Mr. Phillips had gone missing, I'd been glad. It was all over the news for months, and I'd watched every single broadcast, praying they hadn't found him. I'd known he hadn't run away. The man was too sure of himself for that. If someone had seen something or accused him of something, he would've acted like he didn't know what they were talking about, that he'd get away with it.

When months went by without a trace of him anywhere, I'd breathed a sigh of relief and promised myself I'd never say anything about what happened with Mick. Mr. Phillips was gone and there was no chance of him hurting anyone ever again, and I'd promised my best friend I'd keep my mouth shut. So I had.

I pulled my legs up against my chest and dropped my head to my knees.

Then I asked Mick to forgive me for not keeping his secret.

Chapter 16

Thomas

"You're not comin' in here," my brother argued as he stood guard in my doorway.

"He's hurt," Molly hissed. "Let me in so I can at least tape up his knuckles."

"You see my face?" he asked. "I'm fuckin' hurt. Tommy can stew in his own shit."

"You have a black eye," Molly said flatly. "I'll kiss it better later. Now let me in."

They'd been having the same argument for the last five minutes and Will wasn't budging. I didn't blame him.

I was lying in my bed with one arm curved around my chest as I tried to breathe shallowly. When I'd lost my shit earlier I was pretty sure either my uncle or Dragon had cracked one of my ribs. It wasn't broken, I'd felt along the bone to make certain, but it sure as fuck was cracked. Molly didn't know that, though, or I was pretty sure she would have pushed her way in without my brother's permission.

She wasn't afraid of him. My brother's temper rivaled mine, but Molly had absolutely no fear. I closed my eyes and pictured the way Heather had cowered, her arms wrapped around her head like she thought I was going to hit her. I swallowed down the bile in my throat and breathed deeply through my nose.

They'd all thought I was going to hit her. Every single person in that room thought I was going to attack my wife. Heather, who was about a hundred and ten pounds and at least ten inches shorter than me. They'd thought I was going to hurt her.

It hadn't been my intention, not for a second, but I knew it hadn't looked that way. Had I wanted to keep her quiet? Yes. But I'd never even considered using force. Will had been holding me back from her since she'd come into the room and the longer I'd had to watch her freaking out without being able to hold her, the worse my anxiety had gotten. By the time she'd started spilling secrets I'd been at the end of my rope.

It wasn't even the words spilling out of her mouth, though those had made my skin crawl. It had been the look on her face as she spoke that had pushed me over the edge.

So I'd done what I had to just to *get to her*. Just to get my hands on her. I hadn't wanted to fucking hurt her. But the minute I'd gotten past Will, she'd been terrified. I'd seen it. Hell, I'd *felt* it. The entire room had felt it.

That had made me even worse. I hadn't been thinking straight. I knew that. She'd been terrified of me. I'd been the problem. But when I saw her drop down onto the floor, the only thing I'd been able to focus on was the fact they were keeping me from her. It hadn't quite registered that she was cowering from me.

It wasn't until they'd held me against the floor, with a knee in my back and another on my neck, that I'd comprehended what I'd done.

"Will," Molly said, sweetly. "Get the hell out of my way."

She pushed into the room and Will growled as he spun and followed her to the edge of the bed.

"I swear to Christ, Tommy," he warned, his jaw tight.

"I'm good," I mumbled through swollen lips.

"God, Tommy," Molly whispered, gently brushing my hair back from my forehead. "Why didn't you just stop?"

I hadn't seen my face, but I guessed it was pretty bad by the look in her eyes.

"They wouldn't let me get to Heather," I rasped, closing my eyes.

"Of course we fuckin' didn't," Will shot back.

"Will," Molly snapped. "I didn't ask for your opinion."

"Wasn't gonna hurt her," I told Molly, looking up at her. "I wouldn't do that."

"Is that a fuckin' joke?" Will asked.

I shook my head and closed my eyes again, blocking him out. I knew what they all thought and there was no way to prove them wrong.

"Is there something wrong with your ribs?" Molly asked, resting her hand softly on my arm.

"Think I cracked one," I answered.

"Your breathing is a little fast," she mumbled. "Can we get this shirt off?"

I swallowed hard. "Don't think so," I answered.

Will made a sound but I didn't look at him. I was ashamed and embarrassed and I just wanted to be left alone.

"Come on, baby brother," he said gruffly, sliding his hands under my armpits and lifting me into a sitting position. I turned my head away so I wouldn't have to meet his eyes.

"Can you lift your arms?" Molly asked.

"No," I rasped. There was no fucking way that was happening.

I heard the snick of a knife, and then Will was cutting open the front of my ripped t-shirt, baring my chest and stomach.

"Oh my God," Molly said in horror as she peeled the shirt down my arms. "You need to go to a hospital. Will, we need to take him to the hospital."

"I'm fine," I rasped, shifting a little on the bed. "It'll heal."

"Tommy, you could have internal bleeding. This—" she shook her head, eyes wide. "This is bad."

"I'm fine," I said again as the door swung open. My mouth

slammed shut as my dad came in the room. I glanced behind him, but he no longer had Heather with him.

"Ah, TomTom," he said my childhood nickname quietly, as he looked me over.

"He needs to go to a—" Molly's words cut off as Will shushed her.

"My boy," Dad said, crossing the room. When he got to me, his jaw clenched, and he practically fell onto his knees.

My eyes watered and I turned my head away. He knew.

"It's okay, son," he said, reaching out to wrap his hand around the back of my neck.

He pulled me against him gently, holding my head against his shoulder, and when his other hand started rubbing my back like he'd done when I was a kid, I couldn't stop the sob that tore out of my throat. I'd held my tongue for so long, kept the secret for so long, that when it was finally out it felt like something was tearing loose in my chest. My baby brother, my best friend, had been preyed on by some asshole and I'd had no idea. I hadn't helped him. I hadn't taken care of him. I knew him best, and I'd missed it.

"It's alright, son," Dad murmured, rubbing his hand around and around in small circles between my shoulder blades. "It's alright."

"I burned him," I choked out. "Cut him into pieces and buried him all over the Tillamook Forest."

"Okay, Tommy," my dad said, his arms steady. "Okay."

I let it all out. I didn't care if Molly and Will were still there. I didn't care if the door was open or closed, or if the entire club had come to watch. I shook and sobbed and my dad didn't move except for that hand rubbing my back. He murmured and trembled, his voice growing hoarse, but he didn't pull away.

"Didn't want you to know," I said finally, my breath choppy. "Mom was barely gettin' out of bed."

"You can tell us anything," my dad replied. "Your ma and I have been through shit you can't even imagine. There ain't nothin' in this world that'll break us."

I nodded against his shoulder.

"Wasn't your fault, Thomas," he said, kissing the side of my head. "I know you, boy. Know the shit that runs through your head, know what you're gonna do before you do it, and ain't none a'this your fault. You hear me?"

"I should have seen it," I whispered, so fucking ashamed I could barely breathe. "I should have noticed."

"You were seventeen years old."

"Old enough," I replied.

Dad pulled back so he could look me in the eyes. "How'd you find out, son?"

I clenched my jaw and looked away.

"Thomas," he said.

"He had a phone," I gritted out through my teeth. "Fuckin' burner. There were text messages. Mick was tryin' to get away from him, but the guy kept sendin' them."

"Christ," my dad mumbled, shaking his head.

"I found it later. After he was gone. He'd hidden it in the slats under my bed."

Dad reached up and smoothed my hair back from my forehead, his eyes unfocused. "Shoulda paid more attention," he said, watching his hand. "Knew you were dealin' with some hard shit, but I shoulda paid more attention."

"It's alright," I mumbled, grabbing his wrist and pulling his hand out of my hair. "Everything was fucked back then."

We were quiet after that, both of us lost in our memories. The months after Mick's death had been unbearable. I hadn't been able to function without lashing out at everyone and everything and I'd been pretty sure I'd die from the guilt.

My baby brother, the boy I'd wrestled with and picked on and who'd followed me around for most of my life, had tackled me to the ground when the shooting started. He was bigger, and stronger, and no matter how I'd struggled, he'd held me down.

Thud. One heartbeat. Thud. Three heartbeats. Thud.

He'd been hit three times, and I'd felt his body jerk with each one.

There was no way to move past that. No way to come to grips with it. My brother had died shielding me with his body and it shouldn't have been that way.

I was the elder. It was my job to protect him, not the other way around.

Goddamn him.

I was so fucking *angry* with him.

When I'd found out about what had been happening, that he'd been hiding this horrible secret from everyone, I'd snapped. I wasn't sure how I'd had the foresight to cover my tracks, but it must have been ingrained like muscle memory, because no one saw me when I'd snatched Mark Phillips off his front porch the day after I found Mick's phone.

I'd taken my time with him, and I'd left no trace behind.

And I'd never said a word, protecting my baby brother the only way I could anymore.

I shifted on the bed, and it was enough to knock my dad out of whatever memory he'd been living in. He climbed to his feet and sat next to me, leaning forward until his elbows rested on his knees.

"How's Heather?" I asked, staring at my hands. They were so torn up I could barely move them.

"Scared," my dad said quietly. "Upset."

"I didn't mean—" my voice broke. "I wasn't gonna hurt her."

My dad said nothing.

"Swear to Christ," I said roughly. "I wouldn't do that."

He turned his head slowly and met my eyes, nodding after a moment. "Alright," he replied softly.

"She's okay?" I asked, swallowing hard. "She's not hurt?"

"She's hurtin', son," he answered. "But she'll be okay."

"I wasn't tryin' to scare her," I rasped, my throat tight. "I was tryin' to get to her."

"We gotta get you some help," he said gently. "Ain't no controllin' you when you're like that. We gotta figure out how to fix it, son."

"Okay." I nodded. "Okay."

Chapter 17

HEATHER

"I'M FINE," I told my sister, my throat raw from crying. "I just want to go to sleep."

After I'd left Grease and Callie's room that night, I'd found my sister sitting in the hallway, her arms wrapped around her knees. Waiting. She hadn't understood what was happening and she hadn't been sure what room I was in, but she'd known I'd needed her.

I'd walked straight to her, my eyes dry, and the moment I held out my hand she'd gripped it tightly and led me out of the clubhouse and right to her car. We'd left without a word to anyone, not even Rocky, and she'd let me sit in silence the entire way to my apartment.

She hadn't said a word until I'd undressed and climbed into bed.

"You sure you don't want to talk about it?" she asked quietly, running her fingers through my hair.

"No," I replied. "Not tonight."

"Okay." She climbed up next to me and sat with her back against the headboard, and I automatically scooted over to rest my head on her lap.

I closed my eyes as I felt her cool fingers slide across my forehead.

We stayed like that, both of us silent, until I finally drifted off to sleep.

★ ★ ★

"SISTERBEAST," MEL CALLED softly the next morning, rubbing my shoulder. "Callie and Farrah are here to see you."

"What?" I asked, reaching up to rub my eyes. "What time is it?"

"Nine thirty," she said. "I asked them to wait outside since you don't have any pants on."

"Thanks," I grumbled. I'd tossed and turned the entire night. It didn't even feel like I'd slept.

I climbed off the bed and pulled on a pair of sweats and a bra, then waved at Mel to let my visitors in as I walked to the kitchen for some coffee. My head was throbbing.

"Hey, Heather," Callie said as she came inside. She looked around for a second before setting her purse on the floor and moving further into the room. "How ya doing?"

"Tired," I replied, giving her a wan smile. "How about you?"

"Same," she said.

"Well, I feel like shit," Farrah announced. "You have coffee?"

"Help yourself," I muttered, moving out of her way. I glanced at my sister, but she was staring at Farrah in horror as she put a ton of sugar in her empty mug then poured her coffee in on top.

"You can sit," I offered to Callie, gesturing toward the bed.

"Thanks," she said with a small smile. She kicked off her shoes and surprised me by climbing onto the bed and making herself comfortable.

"Make yourself at home," I said with a laugh.

She shrugged and patted the bed beside her.

Within minutes, all of us were sitting in a circle on the bed in complete silence.

"How is he?" I asked finally, picking at a loose thread on my comforter.

"He's—"

"Still an idiot," Farrah said dryly, cutting Callie off.

Callie shot her a glare, then looked at me. "He's upset," she said quietly. "Worried about you."

My sister snorted.

"Stop," I mumbled to Mel, laying my hand on her thigh.

"He's a lot like his mother," Farrah said, leaning back against my headboard and stretching out her legs. "Said he was fine over and over again until he couldn't say it anymore."

"True," Callie said. She reached for Farrah's coffee without a word, took a sip and then handed it back. "When I was young, the same thing happened to me. Different symptoms, though."

I sat silently, waiting for her to continue. I had no idea what to say.

Tommy had terrified me. I had no idea how to even process that.

"I think he has PTSD," Callie finally said. "I've always thought it, but he's an adult." She paused, reaching up to pick at the skin on her lips until Farrah smacked her hand back down again. "He refused to see anyone about it." Callie shrugged. "But he finally agreed last night."

"That's good," I replied scratchily, then cleared my throat. "I'm glad."

"I don't know how much you know about the shooting," Farrah said, her voice uncharacteristically solemn.

"Nothing really," I murmured, shaking my head. "Only what I heard on the news."

Callie made a surprised noise in her throat and sniffled.

"It was bad," Farrah told me. "Real bad. Just another family barbecue, Gram's birthday, and then in the blink of an eye, total chaos. We were dropping, just—" she shook her head, her eyes wide. "We were just *dropping*. Like fucking flies. And Micky," she choked out. "He was covering Tommy. Completely covering him. When Grease got to them, Tommy didn't have a scratch on him."

I shook my head, staring at her in disbelief. Oh God. *No*.

"I tried to get to them," Callie said, lifting her palms out in front of her. "I tried, but—"

Farrah reached out and handed Callie her cup of coffee, then patted her on the back.

"Callie dropped like a fly, too," Farrah said, making Callie choke on the hot coffee.

"Tommy was physically fine," Callie said quietly when she stopped coughing. "Mick made sure of that. But something like that changes you."

"I didn't know," I replied, wiping at the tears rolling down my face. "No one told me."

"I don't know if you can forgive him," Callie said. "And I'd never ask you to. Not after last night. But I just wanted you to know the why of it, you know?"

"No," Melanie spoke up for the first time, shaking her head. "*No. You don't get to do that.* I'm so sorry for everything your family has been through. I can't even imagine what that must have been like for you. But you don't get to come in here and guilt my sister into forgiving your son. I saw him last night. And I saw her." She pointed at me. "He completely terrorized her. My little sister who isn't afraid of anything. She shook all night. *Even in her sleep.*"

Callie sat up straight and nodded. "That was never my intention," she said, looking at me. "I would never try to excuse my son's behavior or try to make you feel like you have to forgive him."

"She meddles," Farrah muttered.

"I remember what it was like," Callie said, lifting her hand to her mouth again until Farrah slapped it away. "I remember how Asa felt when I lost it. So, I guess I just wanted to tell you that last night wasn't your fault. Not at all. And Tommy's going to get help."

"Of course it wasn't her fault," my sister shot back.

"Mel," I cut her off, shaking my head. "Enough."

I wanted to both hug my sister for defending me, and smack her for being so rude. I understood Mel's defense of me, but I understood where Callie was coming from, too. She loved Tommy and she understood him, and if there was any chance I could forgive him, she wanted him to have that.

And I *could* forgive him. I'd known something was very wrong the night before. His reactions hadn't been normal. The fact he'd had to be physically restrained more than once wasn't normal. But the fact he was sick didn't mean I'd ever willingly put myself in that position again.

I'd been someone's punching bag before.

"I'm glad Tommy is going to get the help he needs," I said softly, looking back and forth between Farrah and Callie. "But I don't think I can go back. I'm sorry."

Callie nodded her head, but Farrah just stared at me, a weird look of pride on her face.

We didn't say much after that.

When they left, they took Tommy's duffle full of clothes with them.

As soon as they did, I curled up in the middle of my bed and cried myself to sleep.

★ ★ ★

LIFE RESUMED ITS usual pattern, but I began to think of things as before Tommy and after Tommy.

Before Tommy I could focus on homework.

After Tommy I had a hard time passing my classes.

Before Tommy a quiet night at home was my favorite activity.

After Tommy my own company made me miserable.

Before Tommy I left windows open at night and added an extra blanket on my bed.

After Tommy, my apartment was closed up like a tomb, yet I still couldn't get warm.

The before and afters were endless and relentless.

I wasn't sure how less than two weeks with him had changed me so completely, but the evidence was clear. I was miserable without him.

I didn't regret my decision, not even for a moment, but I did wonder about him constantly. I wondered how he was doing, if he'd gone to a counselor or a psychologist, if he was getting better. I worried that he wasn't taking care of himself. I thought about what the fallout must have been after his parents learned about Mick. I wondered if they'd celebrated when his case was dropped.

I heard bits and pieces from Molly and my sister, so I knew he was okay, but they didn't give me any details and I didn't ask for them.

I also hadn't filed for divorce.

I wrote it in my calendar at least once a week, but I ignored the reminder every time, finding something else to do instead. I just… couldn't make myself do it.

I couldn't go back to him, but I also couldn't seem to sever the connection.

He was my *husband*. Our marriage might have started out for the least romantic reasons, but somewhere along the line I'd started to care for him beyond the friendship we'd started with.

Weeks without him turned to months without him, and I still didn't file the paperwork.

I missed him and the longer I went without him the worse it got. I'd always assumed when you lost someone, you might not ever fully recover, but at least it got easier to deal with as time went by. That wasn't the case for me. Every day that passed was harder than the one before it.

A part of me was waiting, I guess. A small kernel of hope just sat there in the back of my mind, waiting for the day he came back and promised me he was healed.

The only problem was I wasn't sure I could trust him if he did.

Chapter 18

Thomas

I WAS PRETTY sure if my psychologist ever decided to actually talk back to me instead of just asking the leading questions that had me spilling my guts, he'd call me a giant pussy and start laughing.

I'd started seeing the guy just days after the clusterfuck that had gone down at the club, but I wasn't sure if it was helping. He'd warned me on the first day dealing with my shit would be a process, but I hadn't quite believed him. I got shit done. That's what I did.

I'd always seen a problem and solved it. It was why I liked working on cars and houses. If I didn't like the placement of a wall, I changed it. If I saw something busted on a vehicle, I fixed it. Those things were black and white.

I was finding that wading through the years of shit I'd been dealing with wasn't so easy. Just because I talked about the shooting didn't mean my guilt lessened. My anger didn't abate. If anything, I felt worse. I always left the psychologist's office covered in sweat and practically shaking with emotion.

I fucking hated it. The psychologist had asked me to stop what he considered to be self-medicating, so I'd stopped smoking pot, which meant my dreams got more vivid and I woke up yelling all the fucking time. Sleeping was a joke, and for the first few weeks I spent most nights sitting awake half the night, chain-smoking cigarettes on my parents' back porch. Usually my mom or dad would slip outside not long after I'd gone out there, and we'd sit in silence until the sun came up. We didn't talk, but they stayed with me anyway. I rarely slept at the club.

It took months for anything to change. The first night I slept without nightmares, I'd woken up confused by the sun shining in my window and for a second I'd been completely disoriented. That hadn't lasted, though. The next night the nightmares had been back, and I'd felt like I was back at square one.

I hadn't seen Heather.

My mom had let me know she'd gone to see her and that Heather was okay, but I'd known from what she *didn't* say that Heather was done with me. I didn't blame her.

My wife had been brutalized by someone she'd trusted when she was just a little kid. Someone without a background of abuse would have a hard time trusting a person that couldn't control their anger, but for Heather that distrust was multiplied by a thousand. I understood.

Every day I expected to be served with divorce papers, but it didn't happen. I didn't hear a word from Heather, but she didn't try to sever ties either.

It gave me a little bit of hope.

I knew I shouldn't contact her, though. Not yet.

Instead, I just went to work. Took care of business. I sat down with the Aces officers and laid everything out for them. The idea that our club would have an issue with someone because of an anger problem was ludicrous. They didn't give a shit about that. They didn't even give a fuck that I had a form of PTSD. Shit, half the original members had come back from Vietnam more fucked up than I was. It wasn't anything new. It was the fact I couldn't control myself that they had a problem with. It's impossible to trust a man who can't control his reactions and someone like that could get everyone killed in our line of work. It took time, but eventually I smoothed shit out with them.

I spent hours in a tattoo chair getting my back piece done. It gave me a lot of time to think about shit. What I wanted, how I was going to get it, and what I'd do when I had it.

I hired an electrician the club knew to wire in my house, and as soon as that was finished I started hanging sheetrock. The house was starting to take shape, and it looked fucking fantastic. My dad and Will had come by on a few different weekends and we'd worked easily together getting shit done. Will had no idea what he was doing, but my dad had experience and he'd stepped right in like he'd been remodeling houses his entire life.

Lincoln had been right when he'd said the DA's office would drop the charges against me. I got word the night after Heather left. It was a relief, but I'd known from the beginning they hadn't had enough to nail me for it. Mark Phillips was gone without a trace. With no body, their entire case had been pretty much fucked.

It was good I didn't have to worry about it, though, because within a couple weeks I'd started leaving the state for meet ups in California, Idaho, Washington and Montana. Once Dragon had known he could trust me, he'd needed me.

As I started being part of more and more conversations, I'd finally figured out the club's plan for the Russians. It wasn't very intricate, but it was pretty brilliant all the same and if you looked close enough, you could see Casper's fingers all over that shit. We met up with dealers and suppliers and informants all over the west coast, and one by one we either earned or bought their loyalty.

That loyalty had once belonged to the Russian cartel before it had gone tits up. The Feds arrested so many key players the fuckers were barely limping along, and the few that were still around began to find they didn't have any allies left. People flocked to strength, and when the Aces gave them the opportunity to jump ship and climb into our lifeboats, they'd taken it.

The Russians inside weren't finding life as pleasant. We had allies from coast to coast, in every federal prison, and we'd sent out the call. Half of those fuckers wouldn't make it to trial, and the other half was locked in solitary. They wouldn't be there forever. At some point, the guard would relax. Their time was limited.

Things were moving along. Life was happening. We were still pretty careful about big groups of us together outside the club gates, but we were able to let our guard down a bit like we hadn't done in years.

Months went by and the weather got cold, but I still didn't get any divorce papers.

My nightmares started happening less and less. Sometimes I'd go three or four days without one. I hadn't made it an entire week yet, but I could see it on the horizon.

I missed Heather in a way I hadn't even realized was possible.

And I still didn't get any divorce papers.

We replaced the siding on my house and installed new windows before the weather got bad. I spent two weeks at our club in Sacramento visiting the brothers down there and solidifying some deals we'd made with a pair of sisters that controlled the meth trade in that part of the state. Casper and I froze our balls off as we rode home.

When I got there, I still didn't have any divorce papers waiting for me.

Eventually, I stopped expecting to see them. I still looked for them, waited, but I stopped thinking she'd actually send them.

Then two days after the beginning of the new year, almost six months after the last time I'd seen her, a courier dropped off the manila envelope filled with her escape from me.

"Fuck!" I yelled, shuffling through the paperwork.

"Tommy?" my mom called, jogging down the stairs. "What's going on?"

I looked up from the papers in my hands and tried to ignore the twisting in my gut. "Divorce papers," I mumbled, waving them back and forth. "Son of a bitch."

"Damn," she whispered.

"Am I supposed to just sign them?" I asked in confusion. "She hasn't signed them."

"I'm not sure," she replied, walking toward me. "Does it come with directions?"

"I'm not seeing any." I handed her the papers and scrubbed my hands through my hair. "But I don't have my glasses on me so I can barely fuckin' read it."

"I don't see any," she said, leafing through the pages. She stopped suddenly and looked up at me. "Do you want to sign them?"

I looked at her in disbelief. " 'Course I don't wanna fuckin' sign 'em," I snapped, shaking my head.

"Then don't."

"I can't just—" I threw my hands up in the air and shook my head again. "She's done, Ma."

"How do you know?"

"Because she sent me fuckin' divorce papers," I replied flatly.

"You haven't seen her in six months," she pointed out like I hadn't been counting the fucking days. "Maybe she thinks *you're* done."

I stared at her for a long moment. "I'll be back later," I finally mumbled, leaning forward to kiss the top of her head.

I turned around and walked out the door, heading straight for my bike.

★ ★ ★

SHOWING UP AT her apartment was a bad idea. I realized that the moment I'd pulled up. She'd never come to see me. She hadn't called or even told her sister to say hi to me in the entire time we'd been apart.

Maybe she was with someone else. Maybe that was why she'd finally sent the divorce papers.

I had no idea what was going on in her life.

I parked my bike and climbed off, but I didn't move toward her apartment. My hands shook as I lit up a smoke, and I shivered a little as the wind blew. It was cold as fuck, but thank God it wasn't raining.

I wasn't sure what I was going to say to her. I wanted to ask her how she'd been, apologize to her for everything that had happened, and beg her to forgive me. That was selfish, though. I didn't deserve her forgiveness.

It didn't matter I'd never hurt her in a million years. She'd believed I was going to. I'd scared her. Badly.

I stared at her door as I finished my cigarette and dropped it on the pavement, crushing it beneath my boot. My palms were sweating. As I debated lighting another one up to give me a few extra minutes to think things through, her door opened.

Then she was there, standing in her doorway, looking at me like she couldn't believe what she was seeing.

Chapter 19

HEATHER

I'D NEVER FORGET the sound of a Harley's pipes. It was one of those noises, that as soon as you knew what it was, you could recognize it anywhere. I'd heard it dozens of times when I was with Tommy, when we'd be at the club or he'd pull up outside my apartment, but I'd only heard that particular sound a few times since we'd split. Sometimes Rocky brought my sister over and dropped her off, and even though I'd known they were coming, my stomach would do this weird swooping thing the moment I'd hear them pull up.

I WAS WORKING on some history homework when I heard the familiar rumble. I had music on while I typed, but the unmistakable sound was clear as day and I froze in the middle of my sentence on Thomas Jefferson. A few seconds later, the sound was gone, but it hadn't drifted away.

My heart pounded as I closed my laptop and slid off my bed.

I pulled on a pair of jeans and smoothed down my hair as I waited for a knock on my door. Then I hurriedly made my bed. I looked around the room and noticed my plethora of water glasses on my bedside table, so I picked those up and set them in the kitchen sink. Then I stared at the door.

There was no knock.

I glanced around in confusion for a second, wondering if I'd been hearing things. I *knew* I'd heard Harley pipes.

I strode over to the door and swung it open.

Even though I'd been expecting him, I was still blown away when I came face to face with Thomas Hawthorne.

He was leaning on his bike with a pack of cigarettes in his hand, and as his eyes met mine, they widened.

I couldn't speak. I opened my mouth to say something, but the words got tangled up in my throat. He looked good.

His hair was longer on top. Even messier than it had been before. And his cheeks had lost the hollow look I'd assumed was his normal. He was cleaner than I remembered, more put together, less sloppy.

"Hey, wife," he said quietly, standing up straighter.

"What are you doing here?" I asked, crossing my arms across my chest.

God, I'd missed him. Why the hell had I missed him so much? Seeing him was like turning the light on after being without power. Everything was brighter. Clearer.

"I got the papers," he said roughly, taking a few steps forward.

"I wasn't sure where to send them," I mumbled, refusing to step backward as he came closer.

"I've been stayin' with my parents," he replied with an embarrassed smile. "Hard to sleep at the clubhouse, and my place still isn't fit for humans."

"I'm sure your mom loves that," I said stiltedly, smiling back.

It was awkward and uncomfortable, and the only thing that would have been worse was if he'd turned and walked away.

"I'm—" he stuttered to a halt and laughed uncomfortably, pushing his hair back from his face. "I wanted to apologize. For that night—I wanted to apologize."

I nodded.

"I know you probably won't believe me, but I woulda never hurt you, baby." He grimaced. "I scared ya. I know that. I was outta control and I fuckin' scared ya. But I never woulda laid a hand on you in anger."

"You were so mad," I whispered, meeting his eyes.

"Wasn't mad at you," he replied, shaking his head. "I didn't want you to tell my dad. Woulda done almost anything to stop ya, but I never would have hurt you. That was never an option for me."

"You punched your brother in the throat trying to get to me," I pointed out, clenching my hands into fists.

"When I found that tweaker on top of you," he said quietly, "I completely lost my mind. They got me offa him, and pulled me inside, but none of 'em would tell me if you were okay. If you were hurt. Then you came in the room and you were so upset, sugar." He shook his head and fidgeted, putting his pack of cigarettes into his pocket and then taking them out again. "I couldn't take it. I was so out of it I didn't realize I was the one upsettin' you. I just saw you, shaking and crying, and Will wouldn't let me near you."

I searched his face, but there was no lie there. He was completely transparent, both mortified and ashamed, but not dishonest.

"I can't live like that," I whispered. "I'm sorry, Tommy, but I can't do it."

"No, I know that," he said, looking down at his boots. "Would never expect ya to."

"Did you—"

"I'm—"

We both spoke at the same time and then laughed awkwardly.

"You first," I said.

"I've been seein' a psychologist," he said, trying and failing to seem nonchalant about it. "Been seein' him since you left."

"I'm glad," I replied.

"I'm…it's not a quick fix, you know?" he mumbled, tipping his head from side to side. "It fuckin' sucks, and half the time I leave feelin' worse than when I got there."

"That sounds hard."

"It is. It's fuckin' difficult." He chuckled, making me smile. "But I think it's workin'. I do. I'm sleepin' a little better. Don't feel like I'm comin' out of my skin half the time."

"I'm really happy for you," I said softly, leaning against the doorway.

"Yeah," he said softly. "Thanks."

My heart started to race as we stood there in silence. He was going to leave. We were going to run out of things to talk about and he was going to leave and then it would be over.

"The thing is—" his voice broke and he cleared his throat. "The thing is, I'm in love with you."

I jerked my head back in surprise.

"Maybe that doesn't make a difference," he said softly, his eyes intent on mine. "But if it does, sugar, I swear to God I'll make you happy."

"Tommy," I murmured, shaking my head in confusion.

"I've thought about you every day," he said, stuffing his hands into his pockets. "It doesn't matter what I'm doin' or where I'm at. Sometimes I leave that shrink's office thinkin' I'll never go back, but then I get my head on straight and go back anyway, 'cause I don't want to be that guy that can't get his shit together. The guy that scares his wife."

My lips started to tremble as his voice grew rough.

"When I'm workin' on the house, I'm always makin' decisions based on what I think you'll like, even though there's a chance you'll never see it. The holidays felt fuckin' *wrong* without you there. I haven't been able to sleep at the club, 'cause I can't stand bein' in that room without you. You're the first thing I think of when I wake up and the last thing I think of when I'm fallin' asleep, every night, without fail."

"We were together for a week," I choked out, trying to control the way my breathing had grown shallow.

"And I've had six months to miss you," he replied simply.

"I don't even know—"

"Do you love me?" he asked, interrupting me. "If you don't, I'll go. I mean, I'll cry myself to sleep at night, but I won't bother you again."

I let out a little snort as he glanced to the side, a small smile pulling at the corners of his mouth. He was trying so hard to act like he wasn't nervous, but I could see it. It was in the way he held his body and his facial expressions and inflections.

"I love you," I said softly.

His breath left him in a rush and he swayed a little.

"But I don't know how it could ever work."

"We'll make it work," he said, reaching out slowly. I watched his hand as his fingers ran softly down my arm, and I let him lace his fingers with mine. "We don't have to go back to how it was before."

"I can't do that," I replied with a shake of my head.

"We *shouldn't* do that," he agreed, running his thumb over the top of my hand. "But we could try again. From the beginning."

I shivered as the wind blew hard, and he stepped directly in front of me so his broad shoulders blocked most of the cool air. He lifted his arms and I instinctively moved forward, stopping in embarrassment when he braced them on the door jam.

I gave a little half laugh and started to step back again, but I didn't make it far. His arms wrapped around my back in a rush, and his face went straight to my neck, his nose cold against my skin.

"I missed you," he mumbled as I slipped my hands under his vest and around his waist. "I missed you so fuckin' much. I'm so sorry, baby. I'm so sorry."

I felt tears hit the backs of my eyes as his arms tightened and he lifted me off my feet, carrying me far enough into the apartment that he could close the door behind him. He didn't let go of me, and he never once moved his face away from my neck.

"I never meant to scare you," he said. "*Jesus Christ.* I never meant to scare you."

"I'm so glad you're doing better," I whispered, reaching up to lay my hand on the back of his head.

"Don't wanna do it without you," he whispered back. "I will if I have to. But please, baby, don't make me."

"Okay," I choked out.

He shuddered.

He held me there for a long time, sliding his hands up and down my back over and over again, but he didn't say anything else. I think both of us were a little raw then, and neither of us really knew where we went from there.

Tommy was doing better, but there was no cure for the problems he was dealing with. Managing his symptoms and dealing with the stuff that haunted him would be something he dealt with his entire life. If I stayed with him, if we stayed married, that was something I'd have to deal with, too.

It would've been easy to fall back into bed again; that was clear from how easily we'd done it the first time, but neither of us was ready for that.

If we tried to build too quickly, things would get put together wrong, parts would be missing, and eventually we'd fall apart again.

"If I don't leave, I don't know that I'll ever leave," he said eventually, lifting his head.

His hands slid up my back and into my hair, and I closed my eyes as his fingers sifted through it.

"I'm gonna give you tonight," he murmured, his thumb sliding along my jawline. "But I'll be back in the mornin', alright?"

"Are you okay?" I asked, searching his face.

"Fantastic," he said, dropping his forehead to mine. "But I'm feelin' a little overwhelmed and I need a minute to process."

I pulled away at the sting of his words. He'd come to my house. He'd said he was in love with me. Then all of a sudden he didn't know how to deal with the news?

"Heather," Tommy said, exasperated. "Come here, baby."

He pulled me back and wrapped his long fingers around the sides of my head, holding me in place.

"I wanna fuck you," he said point blank, his fingers tightening just a little. "I wanna feel your skin, and I wanna taste all the parts of you that I've missed and I really, really want to slide inside you and stay there all fuckin' night."

I tipped my head back a little until I could feel his breath on my mouth.

"But feelin' this outta control ain't good for me, sugar," he murmured, running his nose along mine with a groan. "And we shouldn't be playin' grab ass until we're more solid."

He pulled away and I stared at him in surprise as he took a step backward toward the door.

"Who the hell are you?" I asked.

"I'm your husband," he said seriously. "And I'm gonna do it right this time."

Then he opened up the door behind him and slipped out.

★ ★ ★

THE NEXT MORNING I met my sister at Molly's for coffee and breakfast.

"Tommy came to see me yesterday," I said as I came in the front door. "And he's fucking gorgeous, as always."

I stopped dead in my tracks as I reached the kitchen. "Uh, hi, Will," I said in surprise. "I thought you were at work."

"Clearly," he said with a laugh. He leaned down and kissed Rebel, then turned and kissed Molly. "I'm just headed there now. I'll tell my brother you said hi."

He walked out the back door and I glared at Molly.

"You could have warned me," I said, sitting down at the kitchen table.

"Like it would have mattered," she argued. "You would have said the same exact thing if you'd known Will was here."

"True," I sighed.

"So Tommy went to see you, huh?" she asked, just as my sister came down the hallway.

"What did that douchebag want?" Mel asked, ruffling my hair as she passed me.

"He got the papers," I told them as Molly set a cup of coffee on the table in front of me.

"Did he sign them?" Mel asked.

"Uh, no," I mumbled, blowing on my coffee to cool it. "He told me he was in love with me."

"That motherfucker!" Mel shouted.

"Melanie, watch your mouth!" Molly snapped, glancing at Rebel, who was currently lacing and unlacing a pair of shoes and didn't give a shit what we were talking about.

"That motherbear," Melanie spat. "Please tell me you nut punched him."

"Mel," I sighed, shaking my head.

"You can't be serious," she barked incredulously.

"He's doing so much better," I said into my mug, ignoring the way she scoffed.

"It's actually true," Molly said quietly, sitting down at the table. "I've been around him a lot. You can actually see the difference."

"He wants to try again," I said. "Without rushing this time."

"The horses have already left the effing barn!" my sister said, rolling her eyes.

"Wait." I lifted my hand and looked at her in confusion. *"What?"*

"Shutting the barn door after the horses are already out," she said impatiently, like I was supposed to understand what the hell she was trying to say.

"Huh?" Molly asked.

"They're already *married*," Mel snapped.

"Oh," Molly replied, drawing the word out. "Right. But they're not living together. Tommy's living with his parents—"

"Loser," my sister mumbled.

"He has a house," I pointed out with a shrug. "It's just not livable yet."

My sister looked at me, her mouth gaping open. "You're actually considering it."

"I love him, Mel," I said softly, shrugging.

"Just take your time, sisterbeast," Molly said, reaching out to pat my back. "You don't have to decide anything right away."

"Are you sure?" Mel asked. "Because my insults have been getting pretty good, and I haven't even used all of them yet."

"I'm not sure about any of it." I laughed. "But if I don't try, I think I'll regret it."

"So, no divorce then," Molly said, tapping the table.

Rebel chose that moment to try a new word, and a quiet, raspy, "Diborsss, diborce, div, divorce," floated up from her place on the floor.

"Oh, thank God it wasn't motherfucker," Molly whispered to the ceiling, raising her hands in the air and shaking them side to side like she was praising the Lord.

I dropped my head to the table and laughed until I felt tears running down my face.

★ ★ ★

AN HOUR LATER I walked out of Molly's trailer and straight into

Tommy.

"What are you doing here?" I asked in surprise as I stopped at the top of the porch steps.

"Will said you were here," he replied with a grin, moving up the steps until he was standing right below me.

His hands slid up my thighs until they rested on my hips.

"Told you I'd be back in the morning," he murmured, his thumbs smoothing over my hipbones.

"You did say that," I whispered back, a smile pulling at the edges of my mouth.

I leaned down slightly, and the minute his lips met mine I was sure.

For as long as he kept working on getting better, I was sure.

If he kept looking at me like I was the best present he'd ever received, and my heart continued to race every time he entered a room, I was sure.

He was it for me.

ACKNOWLEDGEMENTS

Readers and bloggers: You're the wind beneath my wings.

Mom and Dad: You rock. Thanks for all your help…again. You guys do so much for me, I can't ever thank you enough.

Girlies: I love you. I'm sorry that I've been so busy lately. I promise we'll go to the pool tomorrow.

Sister: Thanks for listening to my venting and cheering me on… and proofing with your eagle eye.

Donna: I'll tell you thank you a million more times before I'm done.

Letitia: You nailed the cover. Thank you so much!

Ellie: Hi. You totally saved my ass. I love you.

Toni: Oh, hey. How you doin'? Peas and Carrots.

Heidi: I never would have finished this book without you cheering me on.

Rebecca, Tracy, Amber, and Melissa: Best betas ever. Thanks for reading in a hurry… again. I owe you one.

Marisa: Thanks for having my back, like always.